MOVE OVER, WAX!
The Panurge Book of

In this first anthology of funny stor
years, twelve gifted writers from Britain, Ireland and the USA present us with an attractively mind-boggling array of comic extravagances.

There is derangement a-plenty: from Ivy Bannister's wife-slaying chiropodist, to the homicidal bacon-counter operative in Philip Sidney Jennings' hilarious story. There is plenty of blackness too: a gang of angry women shoot dice for the various parts of a male cadaver in Elizabeth Howkins' *Any Old Fart In A Storm*; while in William Charlton's chilling story the neglected child of two free-market swindlers acts out parental pathology in some sinister TV-inspired fantasies. There is also tragicomic farce from some vulnerable inadequates: Ken Clay's Gibbon-mad Ralph Relph; Jonathan Chamberlain's rustic deviant Harold; Norman Harvey's yearning Colonel; John Murray's friendless woodwork teacher Wilson Fuchs. Plus, of course a good amount of understated venom, as expounded in the accomplished fictions of Éilís Ní Dhuibhne, James Waddington, Clive Murphy and Stephen Wade.

Most of these comic writers are either new or rising talents which possibly accounts for their freshness and power. Eschewing smart one-liners and easy facetiousness, they show us that comedy, in order to rise to the heights, also has to explore some of the depths.

JOHN MURRAY

John Murray, born 1950 in West Cumbria, founded the acclaimed magazine *Panurge* in 1984 and has edited eight of its twenty fiction anthologies to date. His first two novels *Samarkand* (1985) and *Kin* (1986) plus a story collection *Pleasure* (1987) all came out with Aidan Ellis. *Samarkand* was broadcast on Radio 3 and *Pleasure* won the Dylan Thomas Award in 1988. His stories have appeared in nearly all the major literary magazines and in anthologies. His third novel *Radio Activity* (Sunk Island Publishing, 1993) was rapturously acclaimed by the Guardian, Independent and Spectator as one of the very funniest of the year.

He now lives in Brampton, Cumbria, in the far north east of the county. He is married with one daughter.

MOVE OVER WAXBLINDER!

edited by
John Murray

The Panurge Book of Funny Stories

PANURGE PUBLISHING
Brampton, Cumbria
1994

MOVE OVER, WAXBLINDER!

first published 1994 by
Panurge Publishing
Crooked Holme Farm Cottage
Brampton, Cumbria CA8 2AT

EDITOR John Murray
PRODUCTION EDITOR Henry Swan
COVER DESIGN Andy Williams
Typeset at Union Lane Telecentre, Brampton, Cumbria CA8 1BX
Tel. 06977 - 41014
Printed by Peterson's, 12 Laygate, South Shields, Tyne and Wear NE33 5RP
Tel. 091-456-3493

ISBN 1 898984 10 7
Copyright this collection Panurge Publishing 1994
Copyright the authors 1994

British Library Cataloguing in Publication Data.
A catalogue record for this book is available from
the British Library.

PANURGE PUBLISHING
Crooked Holme Farm Cottage,
Brampton,
Cumbria CA8 2AT
Tel. 06977-41087

*for David Almond
editor of Panurge 1987-1993*

Yea, but, said he, my friend Panurge, he is marvellously learned, how wilt thou be able to answer him? Very well answered Panurge; I pray you talk no more of it, but let me alone. Is any man so learned as the devils are? No indeed, said Pantagruel, without God's especial grace. Yet for all that, said Panurge, I have argued against them, gravelled and blanked them in disputation, and laid them so squat upon their tails, that I made them look like monkies. Therefore be assured that tomorrow I will make this vainglorious Englishman to skite vinegar before all the world.

                                              RABELAIS: Gargantua and Pantagruel

CONTENTS

Introduction	9
ÉILÍS NÍ DHUIBHNE *Fulfilment*	11
JONATHAN CHAMBERLAIN *Harold*	29
KEN CLAY *Decline And Fall*	39
WILLIAM CHARLTON *The Television Set*	59
PHILIP SIDNEY JENNINGS *The Widow's Legacy*	74
NORMAN HARVEY *A Man Of Understanding*	87
IVY BANNISTER *The Chiropodist*	95
JOHN MURRAY *Wilson Fuchs*	106
STEPHEN WADE *Abe Poge's Book*	136
JAMES WADDINGTON *A Small Window On Gomorra*	145
ELIZABETH HOWKINS *Any Old Fart In A Storm*	157
CLIVE MURPHY *To Gilbert And George Or Who Needs Enemies?*	163
Notes on Contributors	172

Introduction

To my knowledge this is the first British anthology of comic stories for some sixty years. The last one came out with Faber in the thirties and was entitled *My Funniest Story*. Companion volumes included *My Naughtiest Story, My Best Animal Story, My Most Exciting Story* and *My Best Western Story*. Please look out for Cumbria-produced copycat versions of these Faber gems between now and the end of the century...

Trawling through ten years of Panurge issues I found lots of ironic, amusing and excellent stories but not that many I thought really funny. The comic sense is a highly subjective one of course and things are further complicated by the lightweight critical and aesthetic definitions of comedy evident amongst contemporary British reviewers. Almost anyone capable of hectic one-liners or a breezy rendition of some set piece milieu (e.g. the literary salon; the TV, publishing or film circus; last and certainly the least, the academic-campus scene) is hailed as hilarious or devastatingly funny or mordantly accurate or wickedly astringent or bitingly devastating or devastatingly biting.

Fizzy one-liners and wisecracks about contemporary social mores might be facetious, but they are hardly the stuff of real comedy. In the main they make lightweight digs at weight-free matter, what Nabokov wisely called 'topical trash': meaning that it is all a million miles away from the stuff that really endures in fiction; e.g. real passion, real desire, real striving, real despair, real humiliation, real buffoonery. Hence H.G. Wells' depiction of Chitterlow in *Kipps* is worth all of Clive James' prose multiplied by a factor of a thousand, and Dickens' urchin paid a salary to fling stones in *Edwin Drood*, will stay on in the mind long after most of our wickedly funny contemporary novelists have ceased to be wicked.

And talking of wickedness, I would have liked to find and put in more comic stories by women writers. My own hypothetical *Best Short Stories from Panurge* would have had more women in it than men, but that's a different story...

Secondly, it is a crime in every sense to print oneself in anything one edits. I printed one of my own stories because a) I received an inordinate number of fan letters when that story first appeared in *Panurge* and b) Little known as I am, I am probably one of the better known writers in this anthology. And one needs something to bray about on the cover, otherwise the shops, for some reason, refuse to stock the book.

John Murray, Crooked Holme, June 1994.

Fulfilment

Éilís Ní Dhuibhne

Killiney is the anglicisation of *Cill Iníon Léinín,* the chapel of the daughter of Leinin. Who she was I do not know. Perhaps a saint, like Gobnait of Kilgobnet. Or a princess, like Isolde of Chapelizod. Perhaps she was just the daughter of a butcher, born in the Coombe, moving out to Killiney to demonstrate her upward social mobility, like many of those who live there. It is a fashionable address. An inconvenient, overcrowded, unplanned jumble of estates, possessing, nevertheless, a certain social cachet. It was that which drew me to it, first.

Some people think I came for the scenery. My house is practically on the beach. From the front room I can gaze at Bray Head, spectacular for a suburban view. The strand itself unwinds in a silver ribbon from the bathroom window. It is long and composed of coarse grains of sand which cut your feet if you walk barefoot thereon. I never do. There is no reason to do so unless you want to swim. And swimming from Killiney Strand is an activity which loses much of its appeal as soon as the hulking grey monster lurking halfway along the stretch of golden shingle is recognised for what it is: an ineffectual sewage treatment plant. Shit from Shankill, nuclear waste from Windscale, can have a dissuasive effect. On me, at least. Many people revel in it, however, and emerge from the sea, not deformed, but rarely quite the same as they were before they ventured in. Necks swell, pimples speckle peaches and cream, nipples invert and toes turn inward. And worse.

Killiney means much to me. I have lived there for thirteen years and would never forsake it. Not because I cherish any affection for the locality. The roads meandering drunkenly up and down the hill, the opulent villas perched like puffins on the edge of the cliff, the mean houses marshalled in regiments across the flatlands: these, in their essential lack of harmony, disturb my sense of the symmetrical, which is acute. Neither do I cling to Killiney because it provides me with congenial companions. I live in near isolation, enjoying little or no contact with my neighbours, apart from the occasional unavoidable shoulder rub with the post- or milkman. Some stalwart of the local residents' association drops the community newsletter, KRAM, through my letterbox every month. It often contains persuasive advertisements urging the reader to come to a social in the parish hall, or to join in a treasure hunt on the hill, or to demonstrate community spirit by participating in a litter drive on the strand, all such notices carefully stressing that these events will provide excellent opportunities for neighbours to meet and increase their acquaintanceship. Such temptations I have always resisted with little difficulty. It has never been my idea of fun to spear crisp bags or rack my brain in the solution of improbable clues with a stranger who coincidentally has elected to live within a mile or so of my abode. I am not a neighbourly being, not in that sense.

Killiney means everything to me, nevertheless, for one reason, and that alone. It was in Killiney that I discovered my *metier*. My vocation. What I was born to do.

Fulfilment

I am a dog-killer.

I did not choose this way of life deliberately. When I was of an age to select a career, I was too indecisive a character to be able to deliberately single out anything, even a biscuit from a plate containing three different kinds (1 used to close my eyes and trust to luck, usually with disastrous results). I was, as the technical term has it, a drifter. I drifted from job to job, from activity to activity, a scrap of flotsam on the sea of life. If you could call the confined noisy hopeless office world of Dublin a sea, or life. First I worked for the corporation, which was a bit like working for the Russian civil service before the Revolution (or perhaps even after, but one doesn't know that experience so intimately). My duties consisted, for the most part, in writing addresses on envelopes, for the least, in dealing with telephone queries from a mystified but cantankerous public. After a destructive eighteen months, I sacrificed my security and pension and studied electronics for a year at a Tech. Then I worked with a computer company for six months until I was made redundant. Then I washed dishes in a German cafe in Capel Street, where, incidentally, I picked up a great deal of my employers' language as well as much other information which I have since found very useful. Then, at long last I got what I considered my great break. I was given a job as a folklore collector by a museum in Dublin. I was supplied with a tape-recorder and camera, and every day I walked around the city and environs ferreting out likely informants. When I had tracked them down, I interviewed them, interrogating them on a wide variety of topics loosely related to traditional belief and practice, with the aid of an easy to follow guide book. It was a fascinating and rewarding task, entirely suited to my skills and disposition. It cultivated in me a taste for adventure, exploration and, above all, absolute freedom to order my days without deference to the will of an authoritative, pettifogging bureaucracy. These tastes, once realised, developed in strength and persistence, so that liberty soon became an imperative for survival as far as I was concerned. When my collecting job finished, as it did inevitably and all too soon, I was left nursing the burden of the knowledge that I could never again return to the slavery of a nine to five position, which indignity I had endured for seven long years before my break.

The question was, what should I do instead? Killiney gave me the answer. I had officially been resident there for two years before my collecting job collapsed. My enthusiasm for my work had been such, however, that I had hitherto paid little attention to my surroundings, frequently, indeed, not returning home at night, but bedding down in the flat of a colleague, or in the home of one of the friendly folk who provided me with the stuff of my occupation. But, even in that state of almost total apathy to environmental hazards, it had often struck me that Killiney suffered from unusually severe infestation by the canine species in all its varieties, too numerous to mention and in any case not known to me by name, except for some of the more common forms, such as Golden Labrador or Cocker Spaniel. I had once been bitten by a lean and hungry Alsatian belonging to some itinerants who camped, with my full approval (not that they asked for it, or required it) on an undeveloped site at the end of my lane. I had had to go to St. Michael's for a tetanus injection, which had been administered by an aggressive nurse wearing steel-rimmed spectacles. On another occasion, a minute Pekinese, a breed which I particularly distrust, scraped the skin off the heel of an expensive shoe I had just purchased. Apart from these extreme incidents, every night that I spent in Killiney was filled with the mournful howling of dogs. Any walk taken in the neighbourhood was spoiled by the effort of fighting my fear of being bitten, of planning, futilely, itineraries which would take

Fulfilment

me out of the beasts' range, or of physically chasing off the ever-encroaching packs of curs.

When I had finished collecting folklore and had begun to live in Killiney almost constantly, it soon became apparent to me that the dog problem was rendering life unbearable: not only my life, but everyone else's as well.

My work as a folklore collector had not only awoken in me a healthy desire to master my own experience. It had imbued me with what can best be described as an altruistic streak. I wanted to improve the existence of others, too. In short, I was burning with ambition to be of service to mankind.

Killiney showed me the way.

My first dog-killing was fortuitous. I was walking home from the station one evening, having spent a particularly wearisome day trying to get a week's supply of food for four pounds, followed by an attempt to obtain an admission card to the National Library, where I had hoped to improve my mind with some classical reading while I considered my future. Both efforts had been fruitless. Lightly laden with two sliced pans, two tins of baked beans and a pound of liver, I had meandered up Kildare Street, the consciousness of impending starvation slowing my footsteps. My entrance to the library was first blocked by a stern official in a blue suit, who accused me of trying to force entry without a reader's ticket, and thoroughly investigated the contents of my plastic bag. He suspected it of containing a bomb, he explained afterwards. He then directed me to the office of an even sterner official with startling red hair who informed me in no uncertain terms that the National Library had no accommodation to spare for the likes of me. My pleas lasted the best part of an hour, but were all in vain. The more I reasoned, the stronger grew his opposition. Finally I left, strolling through the reading room on my way out. The porter in the hall did not check my bag, which I found convenient, since I had tucked into it the second volume of Plummer's *Lives of the Saints,* a work now exceedingly difficult to procure honestly but a handsome set of which adorned the library's open-access shelves. I resolved to return at my earliest opportunity to steal the remaining volumes, with the intention of making them available to an antiquarian bookseller just around the corner of Kildare Street.

I refreshed myself after the ordeal with a glass of lager in a nearby hotel, and then used my last fifty pence in the purchase of a ticket to Killiney Station. I was obliged to endure the journey in a vertical position, since I had stupidly elected to travel on the five fifteen, the most crowded train in Ireland. My state of mind was, therefore, far from tranquil or positive when, half way down Station Road, a dog, something like a collie but with a terrier's nose, dashed across my path and attempted to grab my raincoat in his mouthful of bared teeth. I lowered my umbrella before you could say Jack Robinson and hammered him on the skull. To my intense relief he immediately released his vice-like grip and lay, subdued, at my toes. I stared at his immobile body for a moment or two, enjoying a vigorous sensation of triumph. I waited, patiently, for the beast to struggle to his paws and slink furtively away, tail demurely tucked between legs, aware of who was master. A minute passed and he did not stir. The smile which had played on my lips receded. Thirty more seconds elapsed. He continued to lie prostrate on the concrete path. Not a whimper passed his lips. I bent down and touched his hairy back, somewhat gingerly. It was warm to my fingers, but I felt uneasy. There was an unearthly stillness in the texture of the fur. I turned his head over and his eyes bored into mine. Round and lifeless, rolling in their sockets. Aghast, I sprang to my feet. The cooling lump of dog meat on the path was dead, and I had killed it! Never until that moment had I murdered a fly.

Fulfilment

Fortunately, my keen instinct for survival warned me that there was no time to be lost in foolish lamenting over spilt milk. The immediate necessity was to dispose of the dog with maximum haste and secrecy. Observing that all was quiet on the road, not a soul in sight, I emptied my plastic bag of its contents and hid them under a bush. In their place I put the deceased animal, intending to carry him home and give him a decent funeral: I could simply not run the risk of being asked to financially compensate some distraught pet owner. The dog appeared to be a valueless mongrel but you never know. Sometimes it is precisely the ugliest specimens who turn out to have pedigrees as long as your arm. I knew of a charming spot near the sewage-plant where my victim would rest in eternal peace, since no-one, human or canine, ever ventured there, for obvious reasons.

I walked home from what I preferred to regard as the scene of the accident, and placed the victim on the kitchen floor. Then I returned to the black spot to collect my groceries. They, however, were not to be found. Some cruel villain had stolen them. "There goes dindins for five days," I thought, glumly. How could I survive without food until dole day, a whole week off?. Hunger reared its ugly head, not for the first time during my spell of unemployment.

Strolling homewards, I noticed torn slices of bread, scraps of bloodied butcher's paper, in short, the debris of my groceries, scattered at intervals along the road. About a hundred yards from where the tragedy had occurred a large ugly dog relaxed in the shadow of a tree, langorously devouring the last of the liver. "Horrible brute!" I thought, wishing I had my umbrella with me, in order to give him a well-deserved whack. But it had stopped raining and my weapon was in its teak stand in my little hall.

Back in the cottage, I sat in the living room and stared

Éilís Ní Dhuibhne

vacantly at Bray Head. It was black and awe-inspiring against the grey evening sky, but it afforded me no refreshment. My stomach rumbled, a dead dog lay on my kitchen floor awaiting burial, and, once again, rain bucketed forth from the heavens, preventing all action. I hadn't a single penny in my purse. After a dreary hour of staring, I went to bed supping on a drink of water, the quality of which was far from high.

Morning dawned bright and sunny, lifting my spirits momentarily. My breakfast of stale oats and cold water effected a deterioration of mood, restoring me to a realisation of my undesirable predicament. The eyes of the dog, clear blue, were wide open and seemed to follow every move I made. If I'd had two pennies I would have placed them on those Mona Lisa orbs and shut them for once and for all (it was a trick traditionally used in the preparation of the dead for burial, as my old friends in the Liberties had often told me). As I rinsed my bowl in the earthenware sink, it occurred to me, suddenly, like a bolt out of the sky, that I was not, after all, going to cart the heavy dog all the way down to the sewage plant, nervously avoiding encounters with morning strollers. I was not going to cart him anywhere at all. I was going to eat him.

In my work as a folklore collector, I had spent two months investigating a particular genre of tale known professionally as the modern legend. Modern legends are stories which concern strange or horrifying or hilariously amusing events, and circulate as the truth in contemporary society. An example is the story of the theatre tickets. A man finds that his car is missing from its usual parking place. He reports the theft to the police, but a day later the car has been returned. Pinned to the windscreen is a note of apology, and two tickets for a theatre show that night, as a token of amendment. The car-owner and his wife use the tickets, and return at midnight to find that their house has been burgled. Another example is

Fulfilment

'The Surprise Birthday Party.' A man wakes on his birthday to find that he has received no cards or greetings whatsoever. He goes to work and, at lunchtime, his secretary invites him to accompany her to her flat for lunch. He accepts the invitation with alacrity, and they proceed to her apartment. She leaves him in the living room and entering the bedroom, says she will be back in a minute. He uses the opportunity to undress, and is sitting on the sofa, completely naked, when the bedroom door bursts open and his wife, children, neighbours and colleagues leap into the room singing "Happy Birthday to You". In the course of my wanderings in Dublin I had learned that the best-known legend, amounting really to little more than a belief, reported the use of dog as food in Chinese restaurants. Alsatian Kung Fu, Sweet and Sour Terrier, Collie Curry, were familiar names to me. It had taken only a trifle of investigation to discover that it was untrue that the Chinese served dog in their Irish outlets, but that in China and other parts of Asia, dog was consumed as a normal part of the diet.

I got out my carving-knife (my mother had given it to me as a house-warming present when I moved to the cottage: it is a long sharp knife with a bone handle, an antique, she told me) and flayed the animal. It was not easy, but neither was it as difficult as it may sound. In a matter of an hour or so the soft brown skin, dripping, it must be admitted, with soft wet blood, lay on a wad of newspaper on the floor. Then I sliced meat off the trunk of the dog: its legs were fragile and skinny and would be good for nothing but stock. Within half an hour, I had removed all edible flesh from the carcass (I had long ceased to think of it as a corpse). I carried the remains out to the yard and pondered how best to dispose of them. First I considered burning, but decided that the smell of roasting flesh might carry to my unknown neighbours and arouse anxiety among them. I secondly contemplated dumping them into the adjacent ocean. This thought developed rapidly into a better plan. I would walk to the sewage-plant where I had first considered burying the total animal, and throw what remained of him into the cesspool, which was open to the public. The body would be processed with the effluent from Shankill and whatever else went into the stinking hole, and leave no trace to be discovered, now or ever. The plan seemed so fool-proof that I immediately felt happier than I had at any stage of my life since my terrible encounter with the keepers of the national literature some twenty hours earlier.

It worked like a dream. No-one observed me as I plodded along the uncomfortable shingle towards the plant. No-one observed me climb to the edge of the cesspool, and no-one observed me tip the sack of bones into it. Coming home, sauntering along the tide line, now and then running out to avoid a brazen wave, I met a man leading a red setter, and bade him a cheery "Good morning". He smiled genially in response. No trace of knowledge or malice marked his weather-beaten countenance. I had been undetected.

I made a curry of the meat for Saturday's dinner: I had some spices in my cupboard, relics from more affluent days, as well as a cup of brown rice, which I prefer to the white: it is so much better for the digestion. The meal was superb: aromatic, tender, of a delicacy which I had never sampled before in the take-aways of Blackrock, Dun Laoghaire or even China, which I had visited as a student on a package trip. I had some left-over curry for Sunday's lunch (it tasted even better then) and two hefty cutlets for tea on the Sabbath. I had not eaten so well in several months.

The skin of the dog lay in my yard over the weekend. The blood dried off and the pelt seemed to be curing itself naturally. I cut off the straggly corners where the legs and tail protruded. I always hate those bits on animal skins, even on

Fulfilment

sheepskins. They seem so ostentatious as if one were giving proof that the skin were real and not spun-nylon. I laid my genuine pelt in front of the fireplace. It looked shaggy, warm and inviting. I decided that I would refer to it in future conversations, even those which were conducted exclusively in my own company, (which accounted for most) as my antelope, received from a friend who hunted in Gambia, where, I vaguely recalled, antelope still survived in sufficient numbers to be hunted. My friend visited Africa every spring, I'd decided, when the antelope were small.

One thing led to another. My natural antipathy to the canine species, my diagnosis of Killiney's main problem as the dog problem, my urgent need for lucrative entrepreneurial employment, all conspired to persuade me that dog-killing would be my next job. I plunged into it with my whole heart. It was so easy, after all, to find prey. Indeed, it usually found me, snapping and yelping at my feet whenever I ventured out of the house. It was a simple matter to remember to carry my large umbrella, bought, in any case, as a weapon, and to batter any nosy beast on the head, on the right spot just above the temple (death was invariably instant and painless). I always carried a big shopping bag on my hunting expeditions, and suffered few setbacks in transporting carcasses from strand, street or railway to my home.

My methods of disposing of the products of my enterprise varied and expanded in variety as time passed. Initially basing my plans on the knowledge I had acquired as a folklore collector, I offered the flesh, neatly packaged in plastic cling-foil, to restaurants, at prices which were attractively but not suspiciously low. I did not, of course, approach Chinese or Indonesian restaurants. The owners would have immediately recognised my wares for what they were, and who knows what their reactions would be. Never trust a foreigner. No, I circulated the more exclusive native establishments, the cosy wee bistros with which the southern coastline of Dublin is so liberally peppered. I had, on the rare occasions when I had treated myself to a repast at 'The Spotted Dog' or 'The Pavlovian Rat', to name a couple of the better establishments, noted that they served food which was spiced and sauced to such a degree that its basic ingredients, no doubt of the best quality, were totally unrecognisable. They might as well have served *Rat a´ la Provencale,* or *Cat Bourguignonne,* for all the evidence of veal or beef one could detect in either. The inhabitants of South Dublin, reared for the most part in primitive Ireland (i.e. not South Dublin) know nothing about food. All through their formative years they are fed on the Irish housekeeping tradition, and nothing else. Their mothers, bursting with pride about their home cooking, can concoct at best soda bread (the most tasteless, unhealthy bread imaginable), mixed grills, and boiled chicken. The natural reaction after such a diet is to crave the most elaborate messes of marjoram, tarragon, garlic, cream cheese, tomatoes, wine, ginger, and turmeric, all rolled into one cosmopolitan topping for pork masquerading as veal or monkfish doing duty for prawns. This taste is well catered for in every suburban village, if they can be called villages, those outcrops of shops and pubs and chapels which stud the concrete jungle from Bray to Booterstown. The northern Dubliner, at least while he stays on his own side of the river, probably still relies on his native cuisine, that is, coddle. I knew a man in the Corporation from Finglas West who always cooked coddle for lunch. He put it on at eleven o'clock at his tea-break and took it off at one, when it was done to a turn. He gave me a saucerful once.

    The reception I received at first from the proprietors and chefs of my local *trattoria* was not enthusiastic. It was on the whole suspicious. Where had I got the meat? Did I have

Fulfilment

identification? And so on.

It was not hard to procure an identity card. What is identification, after all? Just a card stating that you are who you claim to be. Having to create cards, however, prompted me to use several aliases, something which would never have occurred to me had I not been asked for identification in the first place.

As to explaining the provenance of the meat, I had, prior to my very first visit to the manager of a cosy kitchen in Dalkey, fabricated my story. The meat, I had decided was not antelope, but wild goat, imported from the North, where wild goats abound in the hills of Antrim and Tyrone. 1 had a partner in Crossmaglen who procured the meat for me from local lads, target practising in the mountainy regions. It was tasty and healthy, perfect for Cordon Bleu cookery. Indeed, I added, Swiss chefs prized goats above any other viand. The belief that it was stringy and tough was ill-founded. I would give the *restaurauteur* a sample batch, free, for testing.

This tale, in conjunction with the identity card, worked. It was the bit about the North which added the final touch of plausibility to my explanation. Anything could happen in the North, in the view of Dublin burghers. They had heard of smuggled T.V.'s and refrigerators, smuggled pigs and cattle. Why not smuggled goat?

To cut a long story short, within six months I was regularly supplying twenty restaurants with dog meat and making a tidy profit. I continued to dump the denuded carcasses in the cesspool, but found that I was having a problem with the increasing heap of skins in my back yard: yellow, black, brown and red, they lay there in a multi-coloured pile. I had carpeted my living-room with them, and very fine it looked, but I did not want my whole house covered with the reminder of my trade, and, even had I wanted it, I would have encountered a problem sooner or later.

After much deliberation I decided to shave the dog skins and keep the hairs. The left-over skin I would, perhaps, at some future stage, sew into handbags, belts and other fancy leather goods. For the present, I contented myself with the purchase of forty yards of yellow cotton, and proceeded to make bean-bags and cushions which I stuffed with dog-hair. I opened a stall in a street market in town where I would not be recognised as the goat importer, and most Saturdays and Sundays I could be found there vending my wares to a receptive public: my products were cheaper, softer and more hard-wearing than anyone else's.

Time went on, as it does, and I became more and more comfortably financially, and more and more fulfilled as a human being. I developed my hunting technique, advancing from the simple umbrella to the more complicated sling, which, of course, had the advantage of being able to kill from a distance, and on to the even more complex pop-gun. I began to travel the length and breadth of Dublin, realising that if I depleted the canine population of Killiney too much and to quickly that someone would become anxious and interfere. As luck would have it, nobody at all seemed to notice what was happening, although the community benefited in no uncertain measure.

Good fortune is never limitless, and, like all the most professional criminals, I was caught at last. It happened as I strolled along Dollymount Strand, popgun in pocket, car parked nearby, stalking a large English sheepdog. Normally I did not touch English sheepdogs or other expensive models with a ten-foot pole, but this one seemed to be very much alone. It had an abandoned look in its shaggy fringes and the lope of its melancholy feet spoke of endless deprivation. I felt it would be a kindness to take the animal out of its misery, and

Fulfilment

took a shot from a distance of fifty yards. The beast toppled and fell. Immediately, a man grabbed my shoulders. He was young, over six feet tall, and broad-shouldered. I did not struggle.

"I saw what you just did," he said. He had an American accent and whined. "You just shot my dawg!"

"Why, yes, I did," I said.

"You can even stand there and admit it to my face!"

"Of course I can admit it. Why shouldn't I admit it? It was a complete mistake! Please accept my heartfelt apologies."

"Aw! Sure it was a mistake! I saw you. You took aim and fired at him. My dawg!"

"I was trying to shoot that buoy over there," I said, pointing at one of those plastery-looking life-savers in a wooden box which was, luckily enough, situated close to where the dog had fallen.

"I'm taking you to the police. Tell them your story if you like."

He ushered me along the beach towards a Renault 12, red in colour. Then he drove rapidly down to the Bull Wall, across the bridge and to Clontarf barracks.

"You won't believe what I'm going to tell you," he said to the sergeant, who was sitting beside a gas fire reading *The News of the World.*

"Well?" said the sergeant, with a great show of patience. His name, I noticed from a sign on the desk, was Sergeant Byrne. An unusual name for a Dublin guard.

"This broad here..." ...he indicated me with a flick of his shoulder... "shot my dawg."

"What?" Sergeant Byrne looked up from his paper in some surprise.

"She shot my dawg. With a shotgun."

"What is your name?" Sergeant Byrne asked me. I handed

him one of my identity cards. *Imelda Byrne, 10 Dundela Park, Sandycove,* it stated.

"Do you have a gun licence?"

"No. It's a toy gun."

"Let me see it."

I showed him my pop gun. It is a toy gun. It shoots wooden pellets. The trick is to aim at the temple.

"Well, well," said the sergeant, "and why did you shoot this man's dog?"

"It was a mistake. I was target practising. I play golf, you see, and someone told me it would be good training for the eye to shoot at targets with a popgun."

"I saw her aim at my dawg."

"Yes, yes, well," said the sergeant, "we'll hold her for questioning. You can press charges, if you like. Fill in this and post it to us as soon as possible." He handed the American a form.

The American departed, muttering under his breath. The sergeant sat, reopened his paper and looked at me quizzically.

"Target practising is an odd sport for a young lady to carry out on a Sunday afternoon. Can't you find a healthier way of passing the time?"

"I usually play golf."

"Oh, yes, yes. Where do you play?"

"Newlands".

"Oh, yes, yes. Hard to get into these days, isn't it? I play a bit of golf myself, you know. Up at Howth, usually. Very hard to get into a good club."

"Yes."

"Hm. So you shot this dog, did you? Ha ha! Well, to tell you the truth, the more dogs get shot, the better life will be in this neighbourhood. I'm moidhered with them and with people's complaints about them. What can I do? I'm only human. Now,

Fulfilment

be off with you."

I collected my car from the beach and drove home. It was a great relief to me to know that what my heart has always told me was true: right and might were on my side. I was fighting the good fight.

After my ordeal on Bull Island, I decided to relax for at least one evening. Normally my Sunday nights were absorbed in account keeping, doing the books, as the phrase has it, for the week. But on this particular Sunday I lit a fire in the drawing room and settled down to watch a video: I had a complete set of Bergman movies that I had not watched before. I adore Bergman. The film I selected was *Face to Face,* a slow-moving study of a psychiatrist and her relationship with her daughter, patients, husband, lovers, and others. I was just getting involved in it when my door-knocker sounded. A rare, almost unique, occurrence. I smelt danger immediately but had no option but to open it, since the blue glow of my living room would have indicated to anyone that I was in, glued to the box. At the door were two policemen, who asked me if I were Jane O'Toole. Shocked, I admitted that I was. They produced a warrant for my arrest.

I got six months. The judge said it was as much as he could impose although he heartily wished he could condemn me to a life of hard labour. My offence, he said, in a long tedious monologue at the end of my three-day trial, was the most heinous he had encountered in his life. I had been responsible, he said, for the killing of at least a thousand dogs (in fact, twice that). Responsible dogs. The beloved pets of the citizens of Dublin.

Now I am sitting in Mountjoy in the female wing, engaged in writing an autobiographical novel. Public sympathy for my crusade against the dogs is expressed by a flood of letters from people who have, in one way or another, been molested by them. Even the warders, a tough and unemotional crew, express concern for the fact that several hundred dogs roam the area within half a mile radius of the prison and threaten them every time they leave for a walk or to go home.

I am comfortable in prison and happy with the degree of freedom which I am allowed. I do not have to work and the only constraints are physical: I am not allowed outside the high walls which surround the penitentiary. Inside, I may do as I wish. I am not as happy as I was when enjoying my career as a dog-killer, but I am happier than I have been in many of my other jobs. I find fulfilment of a kind in writing down my life's experiences and struggle for freedom. More than one publisher has expressed interest in my project, which has already received considerable publicity in the media. According to some agents, I stand to score a huge success with the book. It will, they explain, be a matter of 'hype', and already it has been hyped to a much greater extent than any author would wish, and all for free. I could, taking into account the possibilities of film rights, translations, and so on, make at least a hundred thousand. And it will, like all my previous profits, be tax free.

Harold

Jonathan Chamberlain

Harold was a simple but violent man. The turning point in his life came in November 1956, when he was locked in his school classroom for a whole weekend with twenty seven copies of *A Guide to the geography of the Indian sub-continent*. From then on he could always tell you the average yearly rainfall for Hyderabad (35.1 inches), or the mean July temperature of Bombay (86.3° fahrenheit), and even the amount of land used for permanent pasture and meadow (2.6 percent). Rumour had it that he devoured these volumes literally as well as metaphorically, to prevent hunger, and drank his own blood to quench his thirst. But I was sceptical. When I joined the same school nearly ten years later, one of the first things I noticed was that there was a sink in nearly every room, to wash the paintbrushes. At least that's what I assumed. I suppose it's possible that they were added later to prevent a recurrence of such drastic self-vampirism. Anyway, if he was thirsty it would have been easier and less painful for him to drink his piss. I knew this was possible. because I'd read of two German pilots who'd survived that way after their helicopter had crashed in the Sahara desert (mean annual rainfall 0.1 inches).

Jonathan Chamberlain

I first met Harold in November 1967, almost eleven years to the day of his ordeal. I had recently started at the school which he had long since left. It was the weekend and I'd been sent shopping. I passed the bungalow where he lived with his mother. He was in the front garden watering the grass, and although the sun was unseasonably warm he wore an overcoat and a balaclava, at a tangent to his long face. He called to me as I passed, gesturing slowly with his left hand.
"Come 'ere."
I came and stood nervously before him. The watering can slipped in his hand, pouring a stream of rainwater on to the path, which ran under the gate and around my shoes.
"Where you off to, sailor?"
"To the shops."
"Oh, ah."
"To get some potatoes."
"Potatoes, eh."
"Yes."
"Spuds."
"Yes."
He stroked his chin and the tufts of orange sideburns that peered from beneath the balaclava. His grin revealed two bent black teeth.
"They don't eat spuds in India," he said with conviction. "Only rice."
"Really."
"Oh and maize," he coughed. "Fifteen million tons per annum." (I checked this figure later and found it to be incorrect. The problem with Harold's information was that it was preserved in the year 1948 when the book was compiled). He raised the watering can and sprinkled me. I took two steps back, wiping my shirt. He laughed.

"I've got to go," I stammered.
"I'll see you later," he said ominously as I strode away.
I increased my walk to a run.

The autumn term continued and Harold's infamy blossomed. I was returning home from school shortly after the first tentative snow had fallen. It lay in the surrounding fields and woods like leprosy, faintly defining the furrows of the earth and the black branches of the trees. Christmas was near, gently seducing my young mind and infecting the town with its spurious glamour. I entered the corner shop and there he was. I hadn't seen him since the incident with the watering can, after which I had scrupulously avoided his street. He was loading a large shopping bag with tins of dog food. The overcoat and the balaclava were still there, and his neck was coiled with a long red scarf, delicately stained with gravy. I ordered some pear drops and studied the floor.

"How've you been keeping, sailor?" he said grinning.
"Not bad."
"I've got something to show you."
I followed him from the shop, noticing the slight stoop as he buckled under the weight of the shopping. We passed along the high street in silence. Me sucking on the acid sweets and the tins rattling in his bag.
"This way," he said, crossing the road.
The town was small and we were soon approaching open country. The sight of him struggling before me, leaning to his left to compensate for the heavy bag, filled me with compassion. Although racked by reservations I felt compelled to follow. He sang quietly to himself.
"Having a 'eat wave... Tropical heat wave."
I giggled and he turned on me angrily.
"Don't mock, sailor."

His anger bruised me and I fell into a morose silence. My fear grew, but I was still drawn like a moth to the light of our destination. I offered a sweet to make up for my indiscretion but he refused bluntly.

"They rots your teeth," he said with his empty mouth.

Eventually we came to an old fence at the junction of a field and a wood. Harold dropped his bag in the snow and clambered over a rotting gate. It was my chance to run, but I followed, drawn by some demented invisible force. We skirted the edge of the wood, stumbling on the hard earth.

"How do you find school?" he asked

"Don't like it much."

"Can't wait to leave, eh?"

"No."

"Can't say I blame you."

There was a brief pause.

"What do you make of geography?"

"It's OK."

"OK ... It's the most important subject ... Never get nowhere without geography."

He came to a stop, gasping for air. It was almost dark and I could barely make out his face. But I could see his breath turning to ice as it left his mouth. Small silver clouds illuminated by the rising moon.

"Did you know that Sinbhum is one of the major copper producing areas of the world?" he asked, poking me with his finger.

"No."

"Not as clever as you think," he said with finality.

We continued around the trees and came to a halt at the far side. A low moan left Harold's lips. There in the moonlight, apparently abandoned, lay the dark angular silhouette of a large tractor. It was embedded in a rut and leaning at a

Harold

precarious angle. The words MASSEY FERGUSON were delineated in the dim light. The massive chevroned tyres loomed like black weapons. Harold sidled over to the machine and pressed his face lovingly against the cool metal of the engine hood.

"My beauty," he whispered. "Beauty isn't she?" he barked, turning on me.

"Yes," I answered unconvincingly.

"They could do with a few of these in India."

He climbed into the seat and swayed from side to side, hands on the wheel and low mechanical growls emanating from his mouth. He laughed angrily.

"Come up," he said. "Come up."

I pulled myself on to the runner board and watched him play. The air was dense with the smell of earth and the sterilising frost.

"You change gear while I steer," he said. I took the stick in my hand and played half-heartedly with it.

"Not like that ... Like this," he said, wrenching it from my grasp.

I stood dejected, shivering from cold and fear.

"I'm gonna get her going and drive her home."

"What now?"

"Not now you stupid bugger... Tomorrer."

"Why," I said stupidly.

"I'm gonna drive her down the cop shop and splatter the bastards."

"Oh?"

"All over the bastard walls."

I jumped to the ground, twisting my ankle.

"Where you going?"

"I've got to go, Harold."

"Come back 'ere."

Jonathan Chamberlain

I turned and ran into the woods which confronted me like a dark dream. I lurched and weaved through the undergrowth, oblivious to the cuts collecting on my hands and legs. At one point a large branch, invisible in the darkness, hit me full in the face. I began to cry as I scrambled over a wall onto the main road. I continued running till I hit the town and only then dared look back. But he hadn't followed me. I walked the rest of the way home, sobbing quietly and berating myself for my weakness.

I saw nothing of Harold or the tractor till the following year. It was during the spring holiday when I called on Nigel. His father was in the drive, tinkering with the engine of his car. He was a small inverted comma of a man, whose way of talking was at once patronising and deferential. He rose on hearing my footsteps onthe drive.

"Hello there,skipper. And what can we do for you?"

"Is Nigel in?"

"He's round the back. I'll call him."

He disappeared and I stood gazing at the house, drawing patterns in the gravel with my toe. He returned.

"He'll be out in a minute." He continued tinkering.

"How's your new school?"

"OK."

"Study hard and play hard."

I smiled.

"Courting?"

"No," I blushed.

"Remember," he continued irrelevantly. "If war breaks out tell them you don't want to know...War never did no one any good."

"I will," I replied, baffled. I had always assumed that fathers were all for wars.

Harold

Nigel appeared and we left his father, bent over the engine and whistling Sinatra.

"Where are we going?" asked Nigel.

"There's something I want to show you."

We left the pristine algebra of the new estate and joined a twisting side road. The first flush of green was on the trees and a grasshopper warbler was buzzing somewhere in the scrub. We ducked occasionally in to the hedgerow to avoid the traffic and soon reached the spot. As we entered the coppice I tried to recall the fear I had felt the previous year when stumbling through the trees. But in the bright spring air the idea seemed absurd. They were after all just trees and bushes. I had recently begun to question the nature of reality, as preached with certainty by my mentors. One morning I had looked in the mirror and watched my features recede and dissolve. Who am I, a voice inside me had asked. And why am I reflected in this mirror? I began to doubt the existence of the tractor. Had I dreamed the whole incident ? We walked the last few yards through the hawthorn bushes with bated breath. And there it was, in the same rut and at the same angle. But the winter had taken its toll. Pieces were missing and the colour had faded. The words MASSEY FERGUSON now read M SSEY FERGU. Harold? I couldn't believe he would destroy something he so obviously loved. But they had evidently been snapped off by strong fingers. Nigel jumped into the driver's seat and made tractor noises with his mouth. I circled the machine, running my fingers along its surface. I noticed the rear tyres were flat and remembered Harold's ambition to destroy the police station. Since last year he had been arrested twice. Once for poaching pheasants and once for fighting with his mother in the supermarket. Or so they said. No charges had been brought, but there were rumours he would be sent to prison. I was suddenly conscious of the impossibility of his desires, which

Jonathan Chamberlain

had seemed so feasible in the winter darkness. We remained with the tractor for a while, but it began to rain and we cloistered in the wood. Nigel said he'd heard of someone who had been killed by lightning when sheltering under a tree. So we left and made for the town, taking cover in the bus shelter.

A week later I saw Harold again. The rumours of his impending imprisonment had grown and I was surprised by his reappearance. I was with my sister playing amongst the discarded asbestos at the rear of our house. He was driving a dumper, careering wildly along the rutted dirt track and grinning with his two teeth. He pulled up alongside us. My sister hid behind me, gripping my sweater and peering from around my back. My first thought was that Harold was now employed on the local building site. But there was something in his manner which told me the dumper had been stolen. Having no luck with the tractor he had obviously plumped for the next best thing. He seemed to have forgotten, or at least forgiven, our last encounter.
"How's tricks, sailor?"
"Alright."
"Who's that?" he said pointing at my sister.
"That's my sister."
"Shy isn't she?"
The dumper had obviously put him in a good mood. He put it into gear and began to circle us, whooping like an Indian. My sister screamed and ran up the track in the direction of our house. Harold chased after her, bouncing heavily from side to side. I was choked by the stench of the diesel fumes, but ran frantically after him. Without warning the dumper hit a hole in the track and toppled over, flinging Harold into the dirt. He lay quite still, his balaclava pulled from his head. I noticed with shock that he was bald. The

Harold

dumper lay on its side like an upturned beetle, wheels spinning uselessly and its hot engine ticking slowly. My sister was crying, I ran to her and kissed her and she grew quiet. Harold was now picking himself up from the dust. Blood was trickling from a cut in his smooth head and the balaclava was around his neck. He quickly pulled it back over his skull.

"Bugger," he said with feeling.

A group of men were running towards us, shouting and gesticulating. Workers from the building site. They reached Harold and forced him roughly to his feet, faces flushed with elation. One of them twisted Harold's arm behind his back and they laughed. I thought I would cry. Then the police arrived and took him away. As they bundled him into the car I heard him say to the taller of the two that the population of India was three hundred and seventy three million. The policeman said that it was a well known fact, but I'm sure the figure was obsolete. It was the last time I saw him.

My family left the town that summer. I was to attend a new school where, said my father:

"They'll soon make you get your hair cut."

Neither prospect appealed to me. I heard very little from my old friends. Nigel wrote once with the latest news of Harold. He was now out of prison and working as a labourer on a local farm. His wages had been cut for accidentally setting fire to a barley field. He'd eaten a Red Backed Shrike and was to be prosecuted by the Royal Society for the Protection of Birds. As always I doubted these stories, but took pleasure in believing them.

The years passed and Harold became a dull memory. Then one day while reading the local paper, I came across the following article.

Jonathan Chamberlain

> ## ACCIDENT AT FARM.
> *A labourer was seriously injured earlier today when a tractor he was driving overturned trapping his legs.*
> *Mr. Harold Fewrell, 30, of Box Cottage, Badger was rushed to the County Hospital, where his condition was said to be 'stable'.*

I heard later that he survived but would never walk again. I tried to picture Harold in a wheelchair, but nothing happened. Later that month I received an atlas for my birthday and decided to send it to Harold. Before I wrapped it I browsed through the chapter on India. The mean July temperature for Bombay was still 86.3° fahrenheit, and the average yearly rainfall for Hyderabad hadn't changed. But the population had grown dramatically, pollution was rising, and the forest had all but disappeared. The world was dying, but Harold would live.

Decline And Fall

Ken Clay

Ralph had gone crackers before. at the age of eight. It had been triggered by the stained-glass gloom of the church hall his class moved into after the bright neatness of the infants' school, and the fear of chaos which sucked him into a panic whenever the teacher left the room. After the tearful hysteria came the convalescence at home: four months with his mother and his books, toasting muffins on a black wire toasting fork, building skyscrapers with the dominoes and playing with his newts in the sink. Nervous debility they called it then. That wasn't how he felt now but something, somehow was going wrong.

"It seems a perfectly normal testicle to me," said the doctor. Ralph looked down at his pants around his ankles. What made him say it he couldn't imagine; it just came out.

"Why is a fat man like a Cornish borough?"

The doctor looked up in surprise. The reflector, a purely decorative feature, flashed on his head.

"Because he never sees his member," said Ralph hurriedly,

as though anxious to get it over with. It was as if he had been momentarily possessed.

"But you're not fat at all Mr. Relph. Indeed for a man of your age," the doctor picked up his card, "forty eight - you're remarkably trim."

"It's thanks to home cooking," said Ralph.

"Wife watches your diet does she?"

"My mother," said Ralph. "She has a gift for rendering food inedible."

"She should open a slimmer's restaurant. Has it been painful?"

"Not exactly."

"Then why are you here?"

"It feels..." Ralph searched for the impressive medical periphrase, "incipiently pretumescent."

The doctor returned to his swivel chair. Ralph pulled up his pants.

"Well that's a new one on me. Incipiently pretumescent... hmmm."

He reached for a block of sick notes. "Not decorating the hall by any chance?"

"No."

"Sleeping all right?"

"Yes"

"No problems at work? Threats of redundancy?"

"No."

"What is it you do exactly Mr. Relph?"

"I'm an historian." Again that strange compulsion. "I mean I'm a clerk, in the Export department at the Diesel Factory."

The doctor had a bad memory for faces and an even less distinct recall of his patients' complaints. Medicine bored him;

Decline And Fall

it was just a messy form of engineering. What really interested him was sociology; how people lived, what their homes were like, what they ate, what they spent their money on. The card said he'd treated Ralph six years ago for influenza. He noticed the address: Lawson street, it was on the estate. That was the area he most liked to visit — those rooty working class interiors!

"Yes. I remember you." Now he was holding his head between finger and thumb. his left arm was stretched out as if summoning higher powers. "Bedroom full of books. big dog, upright piano, foreign dictionaries..." Ralph was astonished. This man really did care for his patients. It was a performance which never failed to impress those who were tolerant of his vocational deficiencies.

"Bust of Augustus on the mantelpiece in the front room. Potted palm five feet high grown from a seed brought back from Marrakesh," and then, his eyes growing wider as if he could scarcely believe his own memory. "Mother smokes a corncob pipe!"

"Exactly right. The palm tree died though — that bad winter."

"Really? Well come back if it does start to swell."

Ralph walked out reassured but still bowlegged. The doctor scribbled on the card: 'Hypochondria — anxiety induced' and rang for the next patient.

Back at the office Ralph spent an hour in the toilets with the *Frankfurter Allgemeine Zeitung*. It was modesty rather than fear which impelled him to stick it inside his Fair Isle pullover before returning to his desk. The boss, Chief Clerk Arnold Waxblinder, had only recently risen to power and still felt too guilty to discipline an old friend. Furthermore Ralph didn't like to flaunt his accomplishments. He might reluctantly slip into a foreign language if there were no English speakers on the other end of the line, just as he might, if pressed, explain to Arnold the constitution of the Roman Legion in the reign of the Emperor Claudius. But he had discovered in his younger days that enthusiastic monologues on history or foreign parts made people regard him as a freak, a poseur and a snob.

Waxblinder had made the coffee. Ralph considered it foul; it was currently *Mellow Birds* made with powdered milk. He felt he was drowning in mellowness after drinking similar concoctions for the past ten years. But he didn't protest, not wishing to hurt Arnold's feelings.

"A telephonic communication from Jenks," said Arnold putting the kettle back into the filing cabinet, "regarding that consignment of replacement injector components for Barcelona: could you procure the appropriate Brussels nomenclature and inform the Engineering Stores Despatch department of same?"

'Jenks phoned: get the Brussels number for those Spanish spares and tell the stores,' thought Ralph. It was a game he liked to play; to see how fast and how much he could compress Arnold's inflations.

A cup of unusually glutinous sludge slid towards him. Opalescent globules of fat floated between slicks of metallic grey.

"Additional dried milk," explained Waxblinder. "The container was almost depleted, and it is Friday afternoon, so I inserted it in its entirety. A permissible indulgence I'm sure you will concur." They slurped synchronously.

"An unprepossessing prospect," said Waxblinder staring out of the window at the high, corrugated asbestos wall of the Packing Shed. "I doubt if tomatoes will thrive on this windowledge."

"We didn't last long with our view of the golf course after old Dekker retired. This place reminds me of school." Ralph's voice faltered slightly.

"He seemed to wield some strange power over our masters. Under his sovereignty we were inviolate."

"Now we're on our own."

"Until Monday."

"Monday?"

"A new recruit, a temporary reinforcement by courtesy of the Youth Opportunities Programme, joins us in our labours."

"Better than the dole I suppose."

"Well I wonder. It rather depends on one's inner resources."

Waxblinder had raised the concept of inner resources to the level of a mystical power. A week didn't go by without his alluding to them.

"I, as you know, never pass an evening in the week without completing some little household repair, even if it is no more than wiring a three pin plug. I find that the house, the garden and the vehicle provide an unending series of tasks and that the regular habit of meeting such challenges not only saves one a great deal of money but also develops one's inner resources in a manner which more passive pursuits such as reading, listening to music or watching television cannot do. Armed with this capacity for independent constructive activity I feel that retirement holds no terrors for me — nor even the dole, I hasten to add."

"Yes," said Ralph. What he felt most in need of himself at the moment was ten years' solitary confinement but he didn't want to upstage Arnold by saying so. After another hour's desultory scratching in a large ledger Arnold meticulously repacked his briefcase; the *Daily Telegraph,* the Tupperware box and the empty powdered milk tin which would store nails in his garage. Then he checked his Japanese quartz watch against the speaking clock and accompanied Ralph to the main entrance.

Ken Clay

"Poet's day," said Waxblinder as usual.

"Piss off early, tomorrow's Saturday," answered Ralph mechanically.

Since it was Friday it would be fishcakes - one of his mother's few successes. And since it was the last Friday of the month Ron would be visiting after tea. Two beams to illuminate the gathering darkness of life with his mother as she declined into an eccentric senility. Eating was becoming particularly hazardous. He had got used to cutlery with old, dried food on it, and white, wispy hairs in his sandwiches but lately there had been tea made from dried rosemary and lentil soup made from a packet of birdseed, not to mention dottle in the custard and a peculiar pattern of whorls and streaks, like a fading Hokusai seascape, on his supposedly clean plate. After a great deal of thought he concluded that it could only be dried dog saliva. Rufus was a geriatric Red Setter which drooled continually. Years earlier, in its destructive puppyhood, it had chewed volume six of Clarendon's *History of the Great Rebellion.* That had cost Ralph half a week's wages. Further cause for detestation emerged in one of his mother's revelatory reminiscences: 'I said to your Dad that my children were going to have distinguished names, and even distinguished initials too, because that was what would appear on briefcases and signet rings. It was about the time that the Rolls Royce was coming into fashion, George the Fifth had one of course, possibly two, and I was about six months gone when we were listening to the wireless and they were going on about names. And I looked down at Blackie, the Labrador we had at the time, I'm sure she knew exactly what I was saying to her, and I said to her, Blackie, I said, what do you think we should call him?   And she looked up with those big brown eyes of hers, lifted a paw, cocked an ear, and would you believe it!...Barked twice!'

Ralph did believe it, and cursed the whole of canine creation whenever he thought about it. And yet his anger rarely broke the surface; it seethed, instead, under a shell of self-discipline augmented by a sense of personal worthlessness. Occasionally perhaps a steamed pudding covered in salt or the need to retrieve the current *Guardian* from under a pile of rotting fish skins in the dustbin stirred up a tidal wave of rage. And such was the violence of the subsequent quarrel, for Mrs. Relph did not take criticism calmly, that the neighbours might easily hear this student of Goethe and Pascal, this lover of Macaulay and Burke, call his mother 'a scrofulous, senile old slag only fit for the knackeryard.' And she, by way of a response, might label her elder boy, the master of five European languages and the author of an as yet unfinished two-hundred-thousand-word historical novel 'a shiny-arsed, pen-pushing nobody who'd be lucky to find any other woman to put up with him.' Then the waves would subside to a ripple and soon the usual, glassy Sargasso would supervene.

After tea he sat in the middle room alongside Eamonn Andrews bellowing at ninety decibels from the twenty-six-inch TV and read the letter from Roderigo which had arrived that morning. Roderigo answered his questions on *Las Ramblas* and the *Barrio Chino,* recollected the good times they'd had the year before in Cataluna and complained how tiresome his mother was becoming now that she had added incontinence to deafness. Ralph put the letter in a boxfile marked VI. There were five other files full of similar letters from solitaries with similar mothers in Vienna, Munich, Bordeaux, Naples, Antwerp, Copenhagen and Basle. Travel was one of Ralph's escape routes and there wasn't a day of his annual five weeks holiday which he didn't spend abroad.

Ron arrived at half-past-eight. He brought his mother a large box of liqueurs. He used to bring Walnut Whips until Ralph told him how she had found one under the table and carefully brushed it onto a shovel and thrown it in the bin. There was the usual interchange about the kids with Ron explaining yet again that he only had them every other weekend. After enduring a final bulletin on her arthritis and a check to see if he was wearing his vest he was allowed to retire to Ralph's bunker — the front room. Ron had brought a bottle of claret which he introduced as a cheap supermarket plonk. He knew Ralph would see through that one but his habit of undervaluing his own generosity had become automatic. The TV had been accepted as a used cast-off from a departmental colleague and numerous other items in the house, from the washing machine to the cut glass fruit bowl, had been similarly smuggled in. Ron didn't feel guilty about his relative affluence although he had reason to. He was ten years younger than Ralph and had risen cleanly through the academic system. Ralph might have done the same but the awesome burden of penetrating the middle-class world, a burden partially embodied in the list of expensive things required for the Grammar school — uniform, sports gear, satchel - was too much for his parents. Father was out of work then and said that if it was in Ralph it would come out anyway. By the time Ron came up to the same hurdle they were all working. And when father died Ralph willingly supported Ron through University.

It was only now that the brothers were getting to know each other. As a boy Ron had always seen Ralph as a bookish, bespectacled eccentric, fastidiously neat, eerily detached. And since by now he was thoroughly bored with sociology and quite disenchanted with the academic world he found in Ralph a perfect guide to his latest passion - literature.

Ralph's tonic enthusiasm blazed in comparison with the

dreary lectures he had occasionally dropped in on, and what he lacked in rigour he made up for in range. Frequently Ron recognised that the text he was struggling with in English had been absorbed decades earlier by his mentor in the original German or French. Ralph refused to consider these accomplishments as in any way comparable with Ron's academic achievements. He had that reverence for institutional learning common to the intelligent working class and imagined oak-panelled staff-rooms with erudite, quotation-loaded conversations, fuelled by unlimited supplies of port, bouncing between chintz armchairs and leather sofas. Ron described an introverted clique of dreary status-seekers. The younger specimens claiming to absorb knowledge almost osmotically, without effort, while secretly devouring every obscure journal they could lay their hands on: their elders emerging infrequently from committee meetings to damn with faint praise any challengers to their out-dated ideas. Ralph, he concluded, was more like his own ideal than three quarters of the faculty of Social Science. He had only recently learned of his brother's literary project — the massive historical novel. His own creative inclinations, which Ralph enthusiastically encouraged, were crystallising, but the subject was more personal. Ron produced six sheets of double spaced A4, perfectly typed on the department's golf ball, and read:

'I could hear our Dad coming up the back yard, hear his boots clacking on the slate-blue, diamond-patterned tiles, and the ticking of his three speed as he wheeled his Rudge into the coal-shed. I felt I wanted to run for it but felt, at the same time, that I had to stay; it was, after all, only partly my fault. Ralph was upstairs, as usual, sticking pins in the *Daily Express* map of World War II, the one with the silhouettes of tanks and planes in the corner and rows of black soldiers ending invariably with a soldier who had been split clean down the middle. The war had finished six years earlier but it was the only map of Europe we had in the house. Ralph liked to measure distances between all the major towns and note them down in an indexed book. My mam glared at me and said: "You stay there and take what's coming to you!" Dad came in smelling of sand and iron and cigarettes, and hung his big, black overcoat on the nail under the stairs. On Thursdays he looked forward to his favourite pork chops. He glanced expectantly at the oven and took off his bike clips. I had only been asked to keep an eye on Snowball and hoped he would understand but I felt a shiver run through me when my Mam blarted out, just as he was rolling his sleeves up for his wash in the old, brown sink: "Dog's had thi chops Frank. I've made you a nice tater pie instead." '

It was yet another colourful fragment from his growing mosaic of childhood reminiscence. Ralph listened and laughed. The detailed precision of Ron's memory delighted him and he found it strange that even now, forty years later, he could still be hurt by learning of his parents' low opinion of him as a child. It was from an earlier piece of Ron's that he had discovered they called him 'That one' when he wasn't there. The present offering went on to describe his father's gambling and his mother's great gift for the withering nag. Ralph chortled and squirmed and another bottle of claret materialised from inside Ron's mac.

"You always took Dad's part," said Ralph when he had finished.

"I admired the old chap."

"He could be a monster you know; lazy, extravagant, selfish, reckless, dictatorial."

"He had a lot to put up with. She was always going on at him. Christ! Those rows!"

Decline And Fall

"But she was the one who kept us on the rails. We would have finished up in the Workhouse if it hadn't been for her. I've been thinking about it a lot since you started reading your pieces. Your allegiances are quite the opposite of mine even though we experienced the same events. I wonder if it isn't your bad marriage which is at the root of this paternal bias. I realise that the historian cannot fail to bring his prejudice to his material but my own recollections incline me to believe that the old man," he paused for effect and took a swig at the wine, "was verging on the clinically insane, and that if he hadn't died prematurely of pneumonia would have finished up in an asylum."

"Mad!?" Ron didn't know whether to laugh or feel outraged. "How can you even suggest it?"

"You remember his moods surely?"

"Moods?"

"Sulks."

"They didn't last long. He would storm out, bang a few doors, perhaps throw his dinner on the fire, unless, of course, it was pork chops, come home drunk, kick the dog - the usual domestic tiffs."

"I remember them more vividly. They were more extreme than you seem to think. He used to sleep on the couch night after night; remove himself completely from mother's company even to the extent of coming out to eat only at night like a giant mole. We would listen to him grubbing and rooting in the kitchen after we had gone to bed, looking for the food she had hidden, guzzling, if he failed to find something more substantial, whole pots of jam or tins of condensed milk. One such mood, complete with this apparatus of bizarre behaviour, lasted no less than six weeks. And, by way of escalating reprisal, she would take the food to bed in a pillowcase and he would hide the valves out of the wireless set. Then he buried the

Ken Clay

handle of the mangle in the backyard and she cut the backside out of his overalls. Neither of them would even remotely allude to these goings on in the truculent, laconic intercourse of the day. But the great feud. the one which lasted six weeks, ended with an explosion into cathartic violence when he exploited her passion for birds. He set mousetraps baited with bread on the lavatory roof and arranged the seven sparrows he caught in a pie dish and put it on the table saying that if a man had to hunt for his supper after a hard day's work it was coming to something and that Snowball had better look out if he really got hungry. It was about that time that I began to suspect that he wasn't all there."

"Are you pulling my plonker Ralph?"

"On my honour, Ron. I feel it would be a betrayal of the academic ideal to which we both subscribe if a lecturer in the faculty of Social Sciences at one of the country's largest redbrick universities was knowingly misinformed in such matters."

"Six weeks! Wireless valves! Mousetraps!?" Ralph was so deadpan that Ron still couldn't help being suspicious of all this.

"What worries me," Ralph went on lugubriously, "is that we two, as the unfortunate recipients of these deranged genes, must inevitably exhibit symptoms ourselves one day. My natural temperament, I've always felt, has been one of modest self-effacement and responsible restraint, and yet now, after years of virtuous self-sacrifice, I feel impelled to ask where this course of honourable altruism has led me. I find myself removed to a stygian office at the back of the block working for the odious Waxblinder, a man I taught to do the job, and trapped domestically, in a geriatric cul-de-sac in the role of male nurse. I sense the writhings of a secret self struggling for supremacy, an imperious demand to break these chains, to assert the primacy of *my* needs for once.

They had both drunk more than usual and when Ron made the ritual request to hear some of Ralph's own work, a request which Ralph had always denied, he was amazed and gratified to see him produce a green, paperback triplicate book with 'Vol XII' on the cover.

"Perhaps just a paragraph to give you the flavour," said Ralph leafing through its three hundred tissue-thin pages.

'Theobald, marquis of Camerino and Spoleto, had defeated the garrison of the castle and sentenced the prisoners to the customary castration. But the sacrifice was disturbed by the intrusion of a frantic female with bleeding cheeks and dishevelled hair. "Is it thus," she cried, "that ye wage war against women whose only arms are the distaff and the loom?" Theobald denied the charge saying he'd never, since the Amazons, heard of a female war. " And how," she furiously exclaimed, "can you wound us in a more vital part than by robbing our husbands of what we most dearly cherish, the source of our joys and the hope of our posterity?"

A general laugh applauded her eloquence; the savage Franks, inaccessible to pity, were moved by her ridiculous yet rational despair and with the deliverance of the captives she obtained the restitution of her effects. As she returned in triumph she was overtaken by a messenger from Theobald who inquired what punishment should be inflicted on her husband were he to be taken in arms again. She answered without hesitation: "He has eyes, and a nose, and hands, and feet. These are his own and these he may deserve to forfeit by his personal offences. But let my lord be pleased to spare what his little handmaid presumes to claim as her peculiar and lawful property." '

Ron couldn't help admiring the supple, if somewhat old-fashioned style but the subject appeared outrageously arcane. Ralph sat staring into the distance remotely. Ron got up and looked over his shoulder; the page he had been reading from was blank. He took the book and riffled through it; all the pages were blank.

"It's Gibbon," said Ralph flatly.

"You memorised it!?"

"Must have done." He took another swig at the wine. "I read Gibbon every night before I go to sleep. I've read the entire history many times. What a stylist! His prose is a miracle; his transitions are superb. You should try it Ron. Insight and observation may validate the scientific treatise but the literary text stands on one quality alone — mastery of language, the aesthetic dimension; without that it relapses into anecdotal garrulousness. You are now ready for this development. Cultivate Gibbon!"

Ron was intrigued: was it all an elaborate hoax, a stratagem to avoid reading his novel? He recalled the other odd features of the evening on the way home. Ralph was eccentric but this was unusual even for him. Why had he sprawled in his armchair with his right leg over the side and half his fly buttons undone? And why, after having read the label on the bottle, had he repeatedly referred to the claret as an excellent Madeira? It was disturbing.

Monday began with Arnold Waxblinder inculcating the virtues of bourgeois self-improvement in his transient helper from the Y.O.P. Inner resources were his theme reinforced by practical example. The morning had been devoted to the benefits and varieties of do-it-yourself double glazing, the respective prices, the economies of energy saving, the details of assembly, the

Decline And Fall

price of glass, the optimum air-gap, the prevention of condensation and the alternative plastic systems utilising polystyrene and perspex sheet. The new recruit disguised his boredom believing that a good report might get him a permanent job. Ralph worked silently in his usual industrious manner but when Arnold finished and took up his pen once more Ralph noisily flourished a copy of yesterday's *Le Monde* and after a brief 'While we're on the topic just listen to this' read out a half-page article, in fluent French, on the new solar powered steam generator which had just been installed outside Marseilles. A profound silence followed.

"Was that French?" asked the new recruit.

"Time for an infusion of caffeine," said Waxblinder opening the filing cabinet.

During the break Ralph appeared agitated and when Arnold went to wash his cup he poured his untouched offering onto an Amaryllis which Arnold was cultivating on the windowledge. The boy, as yet unversed in the etiquette of the permitted diversion, began to press Ralph for ideas and instruction as a way of heading off yet another desiccated monologue from Waxblinder. And Ralph, who for twenty years had refused to be drawn further than a sentence on the weather launched into an analysis of the philosophy of history.

"It was that foggy Teuton, the Nibelung of Philosophy, G.W.F. Hegel who said that the only thing we learn from history is that we learn nothing from history - an uncharacteristically transparent remark. And this superficial cynicism was echoed forty years later by no less a figure than Alexander Herzen who said that history was the autobiography of a madman. His contemporary. the priapic prophet of Yasnaya Polyana, Leo Tolstoy, defined it similarly as a deaf man answering questions which no one had asked. Personally I incline more to the

Ken Clay

grandiose notions of Collingwood and Vico who see history as a unique hermeneutic device, the key to our understanding of the world."

Waxblinder was beginning to feel uneasy. He scowled, scraped back his chair and went out slamming the door loudly. When he returned forty minutes later Ralph was still lecturing. Now he was pacing up and down the small office with one hand clutching his lapel.

"What then do we make of the greatest of them all? I speak, of course, of Gibbon who claimed no more than that history was the register of the crimes and follies and misfortunes of mankind. Condemned out of his own mouth you might think, and yet it is from him that the spirit of the age, the *zeitgeist,* radiates most purely. How quintessentially eighteenth century is his mordant sarcasm towards Christianity, that pernicious enfeebler of the Empire. He is the English *philosophe,* Diderot, D'Alambert, Voltaire and D'Holbach all rolled into one. And who, at that time, was our class-ridden nation of entrenched reactionaries exalting as the finest embodiment of English sensibility? Johnson! The bullfrog of Lichfield!" At this point Ralph stared directly, accusingly at Waxblinder.

"That lexiphanic windbag! That ponderous celebrant of the dull and the dutiful! That establishment, toadying lickspittle grovelling for his state pension, brown-nosing round the ample posterior of George III! Today we read Boswell while Johnson's costive, clotted prose justly moulders in obscurity. But Gibbon continues to delight; his luminosity waxes. The Roman Empire was the pretext for an excoriating commentary on his contemporaries. And so, even today, there might be, in some hidden stagnancy of our society, another such crystal distillation of the present age and all its ills, disguised, possibly, as an historical novel fashioned in neglected isolation by an anonymous clerk."

Decline And Fall

Waxblinder, by now, was thoroughly shocked. In the past, under old Dekker, Ralph had responded to the lightest touch on the reins; a slight cough at one-thirty was enough to terminate the lunch-break, and a discreet shuffle of papers after coffee in the afternoon would set his head down for the rest of the day. But this! It was grotesque! Waxblinder had rationalised his own digressions as somehow relevant to the general education of an engineering clerk, but these outpourings on history and half hour readings in some foreign gibberish could only be seen as dangerous, subversive indulgencies. Arnold resolved to speak about it the next day. But the next day Ralph didn't turn up.

He stayed in bed writing. The doctor came in the early evening and, after scrutinising the stacked volumes and fingering the bust of Augustus as a boy, suddenly seemed to notice Ralph.

"Ah yes! The testicle!" he said breezily. "And do we now have actual tumescence?"

"It feels like a balloon," said Ralph.

The doctor pulled back the bedclothes.

"Looks normal." He lifted it gently. "Feel anything?"

"No, strangely enough."

He put a thermometer into Ralph's mouth and a stethoscope on his chest.

"Just felt like a day in bed I suppose."

"I've got things to do. The office is beginning to interfere with my work. I know I'm not respected there. They don't understand."

"Who don't?"

"Johnson and his snivelling secretary Boswell. All day long he drones on interminably about double-glazing or his dictionary or the immortal classics or changing the prop shaft

Ken Clay

on the Mark III Cortina while that sycophantic spaniel writes everything down as though it were the word of God."

"A personality clash?"

"More than that. I've put up with it for thirty years but now my work is reaching a climax. These distractions are too much. I need peace and solitude."

"The diesel factory I think you said - Gardners?"

"Yes."

"Well you just have a good rest old chap. I'm sure you deserve it." He picked up his bag and had a last look round. "This really is a damned fine collection! I ought to read more. Keep meaning to. Can't seem to find the time."

"Well I must get on, doctor," said Ralph pointedly. terminating the interview. He picked up his gold rimmed half-frame glasses and the green paperbacked triplicate book which had been lying on the table.

"Quite," said the doctor. "I'll call again tomorrow."

The next day, as the doctor was coming down the stairs, he met Ron. They talked in the front room.

"Do you do much fieldwork these days?" asked the doctor wistfully. "I find proletarian life-styles fascinating. Only last week I had a remarkable case of malnutrition — a building site labourer, lived in a hovel, slept on a mattress on the floor, rat droppings in the kitchen, mould in the loo, subsisted entirely on sausage rolls and Guinness. Quite extraordinary. Couldn't recall when he last had a bowel movement. Now that I admire. The English fear constipation more than nuclear war..."

"How is Ralph doctor? Nothing serious is it?"

"No. Just nerves."

"A breakdown? He has been a bit strange lately. Does he need psychoanalysis?"

"Do people still believe in that sort of thing? I wouldn't

Decline And Fall

recommend it. No, we'll soon have him back in harness with a daily dose of chlorodihydromethylphenylbenzodiazepinone."
"I think that's easier said than done."

"A bit strange you say?"
"As if he'd been taken over by someone else. He seems to think he's Gibbon."
"The long-armed Asian ape? Good God! Yet this might explain the palm tree. Was he disconsolate when it died?"
"No, Edward Gibbon the historian. I looked him up in Britannica. Apparently he died of a swollen testicle — a hydrocele. Perhaps Ralph has schizophrenia."
"I doubt it. What do you think? I rang his firm today. Couldn't contact Johnson or Boswell but spoke to a very sensible chap called Backslider. He maintained that Ralph was deficient in inner resources. Recently he has been giving quite uncharacteristic lectures on bullfrogs, disrupting office routine and apparently telexing sales offices abroad, in Spanish, telling Roderigo he was being poisoned. Bizarre what? I'd really like to see what goes on in those places. Do you ever organise visits to coalmines and car factories?"

Ron asked the doctor to let him know if he could do anything to help, and the doctor asked Ron if Durkheim was still read and if there had been any studies on the inner city riots. Ron left with one of the green triplicate books which his mother had managed to smuggle out of Ralph's room. It was Vol V and each page was covered in tiny black italics. Surely this would illuminate Ralph's dark depths. It was a week before Ron managed to identify that racy scrawl as Esperanto much less get it translated.

Ralph meanwhile had never been happier. As the twilight deepened and the autumn rain battered on the windows he

Ken Clay

listened to the news from Paris on his short-wave radio and spent two hours writing rapidly in a notebook marked Vol X. Then, sipping hot cocoa with milk, but without a skin, from the best family china. he took down his idol and read for the umpteenth time, yet with the same hypnotic attention as when he first read it, chapter forty — the account of the Byzantine Empress Theodora, complete with its hilarious, lubricious Greek footnotes.

The Television Set

William Charlton

Many good things came to the Brickley family when their cousin Miss Wheldrake died at last in her ninety-third year; but nothing gave so much pleasure to young Sebastian Brickley as her television set. This was a magnificent affair. Miss Wheldrake was a rich old lady who had outlived all her friends. She had no relatives apart from the Brickleys, and them she never saw. She had once been a keen goer to operas and concerts; when she could no longer get about, the television was her sole resource, and her wealth was lavished on the latest models and most luxurious attachments. The set which eventually saw her out had a screen a yard across. Its images were of a distinctness and its colours of a vividness hardly to be achieved in the best cinemas. It worked on many channels, and without moving from her chair (an operation she found difficult), Miss Wheldrake could choose the one she wanted by pushing the button on a specially constructed board.

Sebastian had plenty of opportunities to acquaint himself with the television set, since his parents were out a good deal. This was another element in the happy transformation of their lives which followed Miss Wheldrake's death. Mr. Brickley,

William Charlton

indeed, had always been used to having to meet business associates at irregular places and hours. But whatever the nature of his business - this was a topic little discussed before Sebastian - it did not yield enough to buy Mrs. Brickley smart evening clothes and take them to restaurants or night clubs. Now all was changed. Mrs. Brickley looked ten years younger, and gold necklaces and bracelets appeared on her rejuvenated skin. Clad now in a silk trouser-suit, now in a dashing frock, she would establish Sebastian in his pyjamas in front of the television set and whirl off with Mr. Brickley in their new car to some glamorous centre of London night-life. Technically she should have employed a babysitter when they did this. But they lived in a block of flats where there were always neighbours on call; Sebastian at the age of eight seemed quite capable of taking care of himself; and Mr. Brickley was averse to giving the run of their home to a stranger who might go poking and prying about.

The arrangement suited Sebastian. He was not a highly sociable child and the world of the television was one into which he was happy to pass. It could be said that the characters and events on the screen were more real to him than those in the world around him. But it was not so much that he came to live in a realm of images and shadows; rather, the charm of the televiewer's life is that he himself is a shadow, a ghost unnoticed and without responsibilities, in the rich, colourful universe of the screen.

At breakfast Mrs. Brickley would ask about the evening's viewing. Did you see *The Living Forest?* Yes, this week's living forest had been a forest under the sea, with gigantic sea-weeds of various colours, harbouring interesting species of shell. Paul and Hazel had gone down in a bathysphere. And then Fred in *Fred's your Friend* had been visiting old people who lived all by themselves. It was highly desirable, apparently, to visit these

The Television Set

old people, since they were liable to have falls or heart-attacks and lie about helpless for days without anyone knowing. Mrs. Brickley agreed that they ran that risk.

"Did Auntie Rose live alone?" asked Sebastian. The Brickleys referred to Miss Wheldrake as an aunt in order to emphasise their relationship to her, though in fact she had been Mr. Brickley's mother's first cousin.

"Yes, but that was rather different," said Mrs. Brickley. "She was in a block of service-flats, and somebody came in every day to do her cleaning,"

"Is that why we never used to visit her?"

Mrs. Brickley frowned. The chief reasons why they had been unaccustomed to visit Mrs. Wheldrake arose out of Mr. Brickley's discharge from the Royal Ordnance Corps, and the unpleasantness which had terminated her own career as an air hostess.

"Of course it wasn't," she said. "We'd have visited her if she'd lived closer, but Scarborough is such a long way from London, and we had to think carefully about things like train fares, and hotel bills. Fred doesn't have to because he's paid for by the B.B.C."

Sebastian sensed that it would be better not to pursue the topic, but he was not quite satisfied. A few days later when he was alone with his mother he said:

"Were we very poor before Auntie Rose died?"

"Sometimes, when Daddy's business wasn't doing well."

"But once we had a whole drawer full of money. You sent me to get headache pills, and I looked in the wrong drawer and it was full of pound notes."

"But they weren't pound notes dear, they were pesetas, and they belonged to one of Daddy's friends. Besides, you remember Daddy said you were to try to forget about them."

There were a number of other things in his real life that

William Charlton

Sebastian was told to forget, so it was the less surprising that he gave himself up to the world of the screen. His parents, who were genuinely attached to him in spite of their commitment to nocturnal excursions, found it necessary, in order to have any conversation with him at all, to master the identities of a set of real or fictitious television personalities: of Ernie the Earwig, hero of an animated cartoon series; of Dr. Ditherspoon, who looked frail and outdated, but who performed miracles of healing in cases which baffled younger men: of persons who conducted various quiz programmes; and of a cheerful couple called Garry and Linda who accomplished minor feats of do-it-yourself, like mending washing-up machines, which most viewers, presumably, found beyond them.

"Have you ever seen Garry and Linda?" Mrs. Brickley asked her husband one evening, when they were sitting together at a place called *The Golden Windmill.* It should, perhaps, be explained that their night-life, though pleasant, was not exclusively one of pleasure. Mr. Brickley had not severed his connections with business altogether when they came into Miss Wheldrake's money, but rather extended them in a new direction, and they were in *The Golden Windmill* to meet a New York jeweller who might, it was thought, be a purchaser for some uncut diamonds which a South African friend wished to dispose of.

"No, I haven't," said Mr. Brickley. "You know I'm bored stiff by these TV programmes."

"This one that Sebastian was watching last night didn't sound quite so boring. They were making a Chubb key."

"What? Making it themselves?"

"Yes."

"Why didn't they go to a locksmith?"

"Sebastian doesn't seem to have understood that bit, but anyhow they weren't copying the key they had but making one

The Television Set

from an impression."

Mr. Brickley's interest was now aroused. He asked how Garry and Linda had got hold of the necessary tools.

"They found a funny little old Italian, and the odd thing is that from Sebastian's description it sounded exactly like Giorgi."

Mr. Brickley laughed: "Giorgi won't like that advertisement." He had been watching the doorway, and now at the sight of a man who was standing there with a brief-case he broke off. "Ah. That must be O'Flaherty, or whatever he calls himself."

Some days later Sebastian surprised his mother by asking what Auntie Rose had died of.

"Why, old age, dearest. She was ninety-two."

"Dr. Ditherspoon says that old age isn't a disease. He says old people can be just as healthy as young ones if they take proper care."

"Yes, but poor Auntie Rose wasn't in good health, She had a weak heart."

"Was she very fat?"

"Don't know, dearest."

"Dr. Ditherspoon had a patient who was a very fat old lady. She used to sit in her chair all day watching television. Dr. Ditherspoon said she ought to get out a bit more and take some fresh air. But she just laughed and offered him a chocolate. Dr. Ditherspoon was cross at that. He said she shouldn't eat so many chocolates. But she laughed again and said they came from London and were possibly the best chocolates in the world. I wondered if Auntie Rose was like that."

"Shouldn't think so, dearest."

"Why I thought Auntie Rose might be like that was that this lady had a pair of big vases on a table in her room, and they were just like the vases we got from Auntie Rose."

"That's just a coincidence, dear. Lots of old ladies have big vases like ours. Auntie Rose is dead now, so we'll never know what she was like, and it's best not to think about it."

Sebastian found it easier to follow this counsel, because Garry and Linda were becoming more enterprising. The theme of their next programme was the construction of an alibi, now, thanks to the Welfare State, quite an easy task. On the pretext of having a small and harmless sort of mole removed from her left shoulder, Linda entered the labyrinthine ramifications of the East London Hospital system. Sebastian knew something about this because his mother had disappeared in the same way not long ago for the treatment (alas unsuccessful) of an in-growing toe-nail. From the Stepney General Linda was transferred to Ilford Infirmary, and there vanished without trace. Garry, solicitously tracking her, made the plausible suggestion that she had been admitted to the Boyle Clinic, a safety-net to catch mentally disturbed patients who were causing trouble elsewhere in the system. The utmost chaos prevailed permanently at the Boyle Clinic. Strikes and understaffing were the only constant features. Visiting medical students and even consultants within a few hours were indistinguishable from the patients, and often confused with them by the constantly changing staff. It was a simple matter for Garry first to sit conspicuously beside the bed of a deeply depressed young woman awaiting treatment for *otitis media,* and then, in a discarded white coat, to order his wife's return to Stepney. The depressed young woman, who had uttered no word since arrival, was simply known as Leah, and her papers were irrevocably lost in the system. It was a note to this effect, lying on a table in the ward, which had directed Garry to her bedside. Garry simply dropped Linda's papers on the floor, and in due course her admission to and discharge from the

The Television Set

Boyle Clinic were formally attested.

The programme was amusing, but the complications of it defeated Sebastian's powers of description, and his parents failed to gather what it had been about. The fault was not wholly Sebastian's. The rich and newly decolonised African state of Desperia had opened an international airline. Desperian Airways was not attractive to the ordinary tourist, but Mr. Brickley thought it might be useful in his import-export business, and he and his wife were much preoccupied at the time with negotiations with a navigation officer of the airline and a secretary at the Desperian Embassy. The next week's programme was simpler, however, and this time they got a clear idea of what Garry and Linda had been doing.

It was a novel and entertaining experiment in remote control. They constructed a large and highly realistic earwig, about eighteen inches long. It had a little motor in it which enabled it to scuttle about. Its eyes were capable of lighting up. It could be launched by remote control at any chosen target. Linda had put it through its paces by sending it at Garry. It climbed convincingly up his clothes, crawled over his face, and closed its pincers on his throat.

Mr. and Mrs. Brickley did not think this anything like so funny as Sebastian. They listened to his account first with grave and then with rather sickly-looking faces. Mr. Brickley, though he was clever with his hands, refused brusquely to make Sebastian an earwig to take to school. He and his wife took the first opportunity when they were alone to discuss the matter.

"Who are these people, Garry and Linda?" he asked.

"I've never seen them, darling. I suppose they're just people who appear on a programme."

"Are they BBC or Independent?" An examination of the *Radio Times* and *TV News* failed to reveal any such programme as Garry and Linda.

"Perhaps it's got another name?" suggested Mr. Brickley.

"No, I remember asking him before what it was called, and he said it was *Garry and Linda*. But it could be that the real Garry and Linda series has finished, and they've started a new series with a couple rather like Garry and Linda, and Sebastian hasn't noticed the difference."

"Not very likely."

"I don't know. All the television couples look pretty much the same to me."

They put the hypothesis to Sebastian, but his answer was indecisive. "They didn't look quite the same, but then they never do. Sometimes Garry looks a bit like you, Daddy, when you've got a lot of work to do."

"What channel is it on?"

Sebastian was vague about channels because he selected them by means of the press-button attachment. He said it was the channel on the right at the top end. An attempt to activate this channel, however, produced nothing but an undulating abstract pattern, and Mr. Brickley was doubtful whether the button controlled a channel at all. He thought it might be a device for sharpening the image. The only course seemed to be to wait until the following Thursday for the next programme in the series.

Unfortunately on the Thursday evening the exigencies of the import-export business required Mr. Brickley to see an official of the Customs and Excise Service called Inspector Good. A number of these officials entered into Mr. Brickley's life, and they were divided for purposes of family discussion into the troublesome and the meddlesome. Inspector Good belonged only to the troublesome class. For this reason, and because Mr. Brickley wanted to consult him about an adjustment he was making to a friend's bassoon-case, he had him round to the flat. At first Sebastian could not see what was

The Television Set

troublesome about him. He was a fat, stupid-looking, sandy-haired man who said hardly anything and kept tight hold of what looked like part of an aeroplane seat. Mr. Brickley took him through to the spare bedroom which he used as a workshop.

So far as Mr. Brickley was concerned, one of the troublesome things about Inspector Good was that he would not go. He kept repeating things like "Well, it's got to be next week, you see" and "Well, it's Mr. Smith, he's a little awkward, like." Mr. Brickley had hoped to get rid of him before the Garry and Linda programme began, but that prospect receded.

Meanwhile in the living-room Mrs. Brickley and Sebastian sat through *Today at Tea-Time* and Episode 73 of *Space Rats of the Overworld* — an episode Mrs. Brickley thought unrealistic — on Channel One. At last the time came when Sebastian said they could switch over to Garry and Linda. Mrs. Brickley pressed the top right hand button. Disappointment: the only effect was again the undulating abstract.

"Perhaps it'll clear in a moment, Mummy," said Sebastian hopefully. Mrs. Brickley's hopes were that the whole thing would prove to be some quirk of Sebastian's imagination. At that moment, however, Mr. Brickley's head appeared round the door.

"Could you make us some tea?" he asked. " Inspector Good won't take any whisky, but he said he'd fancy a cup of tea."

As soon as Mrs. Brickley left the living-room, the screen cleared. But not into the Garry and Linda show. Much to his surprise, Sebastian heard the familiar signature-tune, and saw the opening dispensary-tableau, of Dr Ditherspoon. Then the scene shifted to Dr Ditherspoon's fat old patient who had been shown a couple of weeks before. There she was in her sitting-room, drinking coffee out of a little cup just like the ones they

William Charlton

had inherited from Auntie Rose. And if it came to that, the vases on the table behind her were exactly like the ones in the room now. The fat old lady was watching something. You couldn't see what she was watching; only her face. What a fat face it was. It filled the whole screen. Rather high-coloured, that was the blood-pressure, Sebastian supposed, but not senile, and not without dignity, for all its fatness. All of a sudden, the eyes changed direction, and then a horrible change came over her face. The eyes widened, the lips drew back to reveal the teeth, the colour gradually changed. From a rich, slightly purplish red, it became a dirty white, with greyish-brown blotches. There was movement, and although the camera held a close-up of the face, you could see the old lady was struggling to get out of her chair. The mouth was wide open, but Sebastian did not think any sound was coming out, and in any case, some loud operatic music was coming to a climax. The thin white hairs on the temples were dripping sweat. The old lady must have succeeded in rising, for the vases behind her head dropped out of sight, and now her hands were coming up in front of her face with funny, flapping movements. The background behind the head was changing. Perhaps the old lady was making for the door. But she did not reach it. The background flashed upwards as if the room was turning over, and then the head, suddenly immobile in a fixed grimace, was to be seen against the carpet. Dr. Ditherspoon, Sebastian thought, would need all his skill to save her now.

But Dr. Ditherspoon's skill was needed nearer home. Emerging from the kitchen with the teapot in this last sequence, Mrs. Brickley too turned white, and with a gurgling cry that was drowned at once in the crash of crockery, fainted on the living-room floor.

Sebastian was upset by this event, and hurried to the spare bedroom to call his father. His father and Inspector Good

The Television Set

were sitting on the spare bed, and between them was the aeroplane seat, the bassoon case, and a pile of what looked like gold coins. At the sight of him, Mr. Brickley jumped to his feet.

"Daddy, Mummy's had a fit, like the lady in the Dr. Ditherspoon programme," said Sebastian. "She's lying on the floor."

Mr. Brickley dashed from the room. Inspector Good continued to sit stolidly on the bed. Seeing Sebastian's eyes, however, regarding the golden pile with curiosity, he said with a smile:

"Chocolate pennies, young man. You've seen them before, I expect."

"Yes, but these are smaller than usual."

"That's because chocolate's expensive," said Inspector Good. "Having them small like this, you can get ten for a 10p piece."

"Could I have one?" asked Sebastian, interested.

"Not this time," said Inspector Good with his broad but stupid-looking smile. "They're for my sister's little girl."

Parents can seem very unreasonable. Immediately after this occurrence Mr and Mrs Brickley decided to get rid of the television set, beautiful as it was, and in the meantime they told Sebastian not to watch it. Sebastian wept at this cruel prohibition unparalleled in the experience of any of the children with whom he went to school. His parents promised to get him a newer set as a replacement, and had they done so at once, all might have been well; but the import-export business is a cruel task-master, and the matter was put off from day to day.

Inspector Good's visit had heralded the arrival in London of Mr. Smith of Morocco, an important man with interests all over Africa. His visit was packed with incident, and Mr. and Mrs. Brickley found their time fully occupied with arranging

William Charlton

business meetings and showing him the sights of London, a city which, as it happened, he had never previously seen. Sebastian, therefore, was left very much on his own in the flat. It was a severe ordeal not to switch on the television, particularly because shortly after Mr. Smith's arrival, Mr. O'Flaherty met with a fatal accident, and since he had apparently expressed the wish to be buried privately at sea, his remains were stored in the spare bedroom in three cardboard boxes labelled *Tractor headlights: for export to Rosslare*. Sebastian felt that these cardboard boxes radiated a certain gloom over the flat, a gloom only partly relieved by a large paper parcel containing a cheerful picture of sunflowers, which Mr. Smith intended taking back with him to Morocco.

Small wonder, then, that as the shadows lengthened on Thursday evening, Sebastian's thoughts turned to Garry and Linda. What would they be doing this week? Their feats of efficiency were cumulative, and Sebastian could not help suspecting that the cleverly reproduced Chubb key, Linda's alibi, and the ingenious giant earwig, were destined to some collective use. Had he missed it last week? Or was the programme deferred to today?

It was a warm evening in September. That, no doubt, was why the air seemed a little heavy in the direction of the spare bedroom, and why the sombre drone of the blue-bottle was becoming obtrusive in the silence. But without considering these natural causes, Sebastian withdrew into the living-room and, telling himself that his parents had asked for it, plugged in the set and pressed the top right-hand button.

The set played none of its undulating abstract tricks on him. He got a picture at once, and rejoiced to find he had missed none of Garry's and Linda's adventures. The first shots showed Garry, looking more than ever like his father, establishing his presence as an agitated husband at the Boyle Clinic after the

The Television Set

removal of Leah. No, the sister in charge was away, and the acting sister did not know where his wife had gone: probably to the Romford Radiatric Unit. Then he saw Linda driving along the motorway in an inconspicuous *Fujitsubo,* just like one of the newer cars they had had during his father's used-car-dealing period. Linda was a bit muffled up, and he could not see her face even when she stopped for petrol at a busy Services, but it must, of course, be she. She turned off the motorway and arrived at a town which Sebastian did not identify, but which was by the sea. She parked her car with some other cars on the sea-front, and walked a short distance to an expensive-looking block of flats. There was nobody about. Avoiding the lift she went up a couple of flights of stairs, and let herself with a key into one of the flats. The sound of operatic music came out as she opened the door.

And then, oddly, the scene changed. Instead of showing what Linda did next, the screen showed an empty room. At first Sebastian thought it was the room of the old lady in the Dr. Ditherspoon series, because there was a pair of vases like hers on the table. But no, it was different from that room, and yet it was familiar. Why, it was just like the very room he was sitting in. In fact it was that room. Their flat was on the television. The world of television had reached out and embraced them. Directly facing him was the chair in which he always sat. Wouldn't it be odd if he himself appeared on the television? But at present the room was empty.

But now the door was opening. There was a little flicker or jump in the sequence, and the next moment there was a boy of about eight sitting in the chair. Yes, it was himself. The face was lit up with a rather ghastly light, but he recognised it easily. It was like looking in a mirror. He thought if he moved his head, the other head would move too. But perhaps the eyes were too intent on what was before them. They were watching,

William Charlton

Sebastian thought, a television programme. That was where the ghastly light was coming from. His other self was completely intent on that.

But Sebastian could see beyond his other self to the door. The door was opening again. Now it was shutting again, and yet nothing had come in. Oh yes, something had come in. It must have crept in below where the chair cut off Sebastian's view of the doorway, and crawled along the floor to behind where his other self was sitting. For there was something now rising behind the that chair. It was a big, dark brown thing, like a gigantic insect, like a hideous travesty of Ernie the Earwig, with black things coming out of it which reached down towards the self in the chair, and eyes which began to glow. Why did not the self in the chair turn round? He must turn quickly or...

All this time Sebastian's own eyes had been glued to the screen, as if by magic. Now suddenly the spell broke. Did he sense something hanging over him? He turned quickly in his chair, half rose and ...

And several hours later Mr. and Mrs. Brickley, accompanied by Mr. Smith and his interpreter, returned to the flat. To their surprise, they found the flat door ajar. Mr. Smith looked disapproving. His interpreter, a large African lady, said:

"Mr. Smith say, is better, when you have much merchandise, keep door lock."

"But Sebastian is usually so careful, Mr. Smith," said Mrs. Brickley, with a quick maternal loyalty. "I can't think why he forgot this time."

Mr. Smith strode ahead of her into the living room, and frowned again.

"Mr. Smith say," explained the interpreter, "is not careful tonight. He fool with de television, make de big mess."

The Television Set

It was a mess indeed which met the appalled gaze of Sebastian's parents. The television set seemed to have exploded under some terrible force. Fragments of the screen were everywhere, the chair was blackened, the two large vases on the table nearby had fallen and broken in their fall, the push-button attachment had melted into an ugly blob. In the middle of the wreckage lay Sebastian. Mrs. Brickley plunged forwards him. Then she stopped and backed away, screaming. Out of the ruptured belly of the television set crawled a monstrous earwig, eighteen inches long.

"You said you'd destroyed it," gasped Mr. Brickley, backing also.

"I did," screamed Mrs. Brickley. "I did. It's come back."

The uproar disturbed Mr. Smith. In another moment the whole block of flats would be roused and telephoning the police. Mr. Smith did not wish to meet the police. He found them meddlesome. The Brickleys he had now diagnosed as troublesome. He always carried with him means of dealing with people who were troublesome. The racket the Brickleys were making came to an end with two well-silenced plops. Waiting only for his interpreter to pick up the brown paper parcel with the sunflower picture, he strode smartly out of the flat and down to his waiting taxi.

The interpreter needed no prompting to convey his wishes to the taxi-driver.

"Desperian Embassy, as quickly as possible."

The Widow's Legacy

Philip Sidney Jennings

After Dad died and my ugly sisters ran away to breed with strange men in towns far away from our little bungalow just outside Eastbourne, I stayed at home with Mum.

I wasn't unhappy with her. In many ways I substituted for Dad. In the evening I ate a hot cooked meal and all I had to say to make Mum's eyes glow with pleasure, was: "Mum, Mum, that was really good." It wasn't hard to muster enthusiasm for food I was used to. Sometimes if I belched after a meal and Mum was in a good mood, she'd say: "Showing appreciation are we!" Then I'd grin. Sometimes if I belched like a donkey braying, which I do unaccountably sometimes, her small pretty face would become smaller and she'd say, fairly mildly: "Oh Bob, you're not sick are you?" She dreaded sickness as much as bad manners, perhaps even more.

"Sorry Mum," I'd say, "it just came out."

"Well put it back where it came from."

I tried to imagine putting a jet of stale exhaled air back in the place it came from. I laughed. Mum was grimly pleased that I was laughing at her joke. Actually I wasn't. I was laughing at myself but I would never be able to explain that to

The Widow's Legacy

Mum, so I didn't try.

Sometimes, like Dad, I offered to wash up and make tea after the evening meal, but Mum wouldn't hear of it.

"No, that's all right Bob, I appreciate your asking."

I knew then she was praising my good manners. I thanked her and went in to our tiny neat lounge and switched on the huge colour television. By and by Mum would come in and with a few quick nervous glances around the room, she would seat herself in front of the screen and bring out her knitting.

She knitted sweaters and jumpers and pull-overs for me and because I had so many and because I was loyal to her I wore one of them every day of the year whatever the weather. I knew this pleased her and I wanted to please her. It made me sad to see her face grow older and smaller. I was thirty and looked twenty. I didn't have a care in the world.

In the years Mum and I lived together I learnt her likes and dislikes through watching television. If girls in strange dresses came on the screen and did high kicks with long legs so that just a small piece of glittering sequined material was visible between their legs, Mum yawned and said: "Isn't there anything else on Bob?"

Immediately I got up and found new channels. Sometimes a drama. Unfortunately these dramas did not often please her because so often the protagonists would kiss and suggest going to bed with each other. This made us both very uncomfortable. I had the odd feeling that Mum was looking at me out of the corner of her eye. She probably wasn't but I felt she might be. I rubbed my hands over my smooth pink face and peered at her, unseen, through my tent of fingers. Her face changed visibly. Lines were more clearly defined. She crashed through gears until she flew in fourth:

"That's it, that's it. That's all they think about. Sex! I don't know what the world's coming to. They've got one thing on their mind. Filth! They've hardly got their nappies off and..."

Philip Sidney Jennings

I won't go on from here to repeat everything she said because she so often repeated herself and like a great public orator she could talk non-stop, drawing energy from her first sentence to build her second and from her second to dart to her third and from her third to her fourth... I felt innocent and safe because I was sitting in the armchair with my slippers on and certainly I wasn't kissing anyone or making wanton suggestions. I got up and found another channel while Mum's words raced on and on with an undeniable vigour. It wasn't her night. A pretty blond girl with pouting lips was advertising a clean white bra while a choir sang songs of the ecstasy of angels. I was almost touched in some strange way but a glance at Mum and I was myself again. Her little face was pulled as tight as a single knot. Could I unpick it with a kiss on her paper cheek? I knew I couldn't. Sometimes my heart raced and thumped and I saw hands beyond my own, hands that picked and pulled at her until her face was back in shape and she was giggling like a tickled girl. She was sensitive. Often she noticed my invisible hands.

"Are you all right Bob?"

I nodded.

"Just a bit tired. On my feet all day. Seems like people think it's Christmas already."

I'd worked on the meat counter at Sainsbury's for the last eight years. I enjoyed the work, the smell of salami, the efficient hiss of the bacon slicer, the feeling that I was at the centre of our small commercial plaza.

"Well, you get an early night. I'll put a bottle in your bed. I'll make a cup of tea."

Often she'd insist on making a cup of tea just as her favourite programme, *Coronation Street*, was about to start. I'd plead with her not to, but to no avail.

"I'm sick of all these scroungers," she said, "never done a day's work in their lives."

The Widow's Legacy

I wasn't quite sure who she meant but it was enough to know it wasn't me and that I did a day's work six days a week.

Over the years I learnt that Mum's favourite programme was really the news and not *Coronation Street*. At nine or ten or whenever it came on, she sat bolt upright and I waited for her character to bloom. It always did. I was never once disappointed. Sometimes I was a little afraid. Mum was so convincing I thought the world might end there and then in the little lounge. Sometimes I even thought the news was in some way I couldn't explain, tailor-made for her. Often there was a strike: miners, steel workers, factory workers ...

"They don't want to bloody work!"

"Mum," I said, referring as she knew to her expletive, bloody. She excused herself quickly.

"It makes you sick. No wonder the country's in the state it is. What would happen if we all went on strike?"

My mind stopped as I suddenly contemplated this incredible concept. I saw invisible hands in front of me grasping for an answer. I saw headlines in newspapers and on T.V. "The World is on strike. There is nothing to say tonight." But that couldn't be right because the papers and T.V. would be on strike. In fact would we know if there was a strike or not? Perhaps people would even stop speaking to each other. Silence and inertia would reign supreme. Mum's knitting needles clicked and brought me back to our world. Then she was on her feet with a sudden cry:

"Bring back the birch!"

I glanced at her, then back to the screen. It showed the shaven head of an old woman who'd been attacked and beaten by two teenagers. The woman's head was stitched and sewn up like a football. It was a truly ugly sight. Mum said the world was coming to an end.

"Birched! These things never used to happen. Animals. They're animals. Look at that! And, my God, would you believe it, they got two pounds and thirty pence from her pension. I'm glad I'm not young any more. If they knew they'd get birched ..."

Mum went on and on even after Val Doonican was crooning a sweet song into the room. He smiled like a flower from the roots of his polo-neck sweater.

"We can't just let the Russians walk up to our doorsteps ..."

Perhaps I'd fallen asleep. The news was on again. Smartly dressed men were escorting long pointed missiles on a walk somewhere.

"Communists! Red blighters. They'll never get me. Look at the world!"

I did and I was amazed. When Mum said 'communists' I thought of Kermit the Frog, Mickey the Mouse and Donald the Duck and if we didn't watch it in some way we'd be Broody the Bear, Ivan the Eagle or a bulldog or lion or something. I realized we all had to be careful.

November became December and I couldn't help but notice that all the tragedies in the world happen in this Christmas month. Planes crash, ships sink, little innocent children develop strange incurable diseases, floods roar and sweep away distant villages, volcanoes dormant all the year choose this time to shrug their shoulders and rage with fire ...

'Her head had been removed and was found with her hands fifty yards away in a septic tank. It is believed her attacker ...'

"Bring back the birch! These animals don't like it when they get a taste of their own medicine. If they knew what they were going to get, they'd think twice. These Arabs have got the right idea, cut their hands off..."

Mum was off again, racing round and round a track of words. Sometimes I tried to keep up with what she was saying but she was too fast for me. In my armchair I suddenly felt sick and giddy as though without moving I was being propelled at an incredible rate. I never could stand fairground cars and fast

The Widow's Legacy

sorts of things, things that go round and round, faster and faster, until all is lost in speed and vortex and you somehow don't exist or you're completely different, maybe even a communist.

She shook her little knotted head at an earthquake and spoke sadly:

"Well Bob, there's so many people over there. It's Mother Nature's way of keeping the population down... oh my God, would you believe that, robbed and beaten in his wheelchair..."

I looked across at Mum and suddenly I saw her tied up in an armchair about to be tortured by two youths. I come through the door with my arms innocently full of groceries. I've just put in another hard day's work at the shop. Wham! The ugly youth knocks me to the floor. He stoops to pick me and I stove in the part of his head above the eyebrow with a family-size tin of baked beans. The other youth, also ugly, tries to jump on my face, but quick as a flash I roll over, up-end him with a hard salami and before he can get up I give him the same treatment his friend got, though this time I use a tin of tomatoes. I turn to Mum and release her from her bondage. Gently I massage the circulation back into her old wrists. She smiles at me with all the love in the world.

"I'll make us a nice cup of tea now. I expect we can both do with one."

Pretty soon people hear about what's happened and congratulations and cheques are flooding through the door. Then the Queen hears about it and I get a medal for bravery and appear on television with my arm around Mum.

I always eat three thin slates of toast piled high with home-made marmalade in the morning, then I'm off to my shop in the plaza. It's only a short walk, down the lane, through a little wood, across a thin field and into the shopping centre, where now a tall Christmas tree towers and makes the world look

Philip Sidney Jennings

exciting with coloured lights. I pause in front of 'Amp and Watts', the newest shop in the plaza and a great palace of electrical gadgets. My eyes are drawn immediately to a device described as The Automatic Tea Maker. Suddenly I know that this is what I'll get Mum for Christmas. We can have it in the lounge and she won't have to get up and make tea just as her favourite programme's about to begin. That'll fool her. I can't help but grin.

At lunchtime I enter the gleaming shop and a big man in a suit with a small confident moustache approaches me. He looks tired and cruel.

"The tea-maker," I say.

"You're lucky," he says, "there's just one left."

He walks away and I follow after him. We reach the tea-maker at the back of the shop and it's sitting prettily on top of its box. I touch its smoothness and symmetry. It's beautiful. A doubt enters my mind.

"Is it hard to use?"

"Hard to use! Plug it in, tea in there, water in there, milk in there, that's it. If it was hard to use I wouldn't have sold out."

I feel a bit ashamed and not sure what to say next.

"We can gift-wrap it, deliver it to your door, you're local aren't you, well no problem, it's part of the service. If you want to think about it I can't guarantee it'll be here much longer the way things are going this Christmas."

"Would you put a huge pink bow on it?"

"I'll put three if you like."

I see from the plastic badge in his lapel that his name is Reggie. I suddenly like him and grin.

"Three pink bows then."

I went back to work with a generous sense of achievement.

In the evening the parcel was waiting at home complete with three pink bows as fine as little pigs' tails. I beamed. Mum was grim.

The Widow's Legacy

"Were you expecting this? It's not a bomb is it? I noticed it rattled."

I picked it up and carried it with a mysterious grin into my room.

In the evening after our meal and the washing up was done I dozed in front of the television with Mum. I must have fallen asleep because suddenly I was awake with a start.

"Cowards! They pick on the old ones. Those that can't defend themselves ..."

She paused for a moment silently changing gear but in that silence I distinctly heard the nostalgic swish of the birch as it rippled the backs of the guilty.

"... You can't walk the streets in daylight let alone at night, Aida down the lane said she saw two youths ..."

My eyes were closed again. I saw myself walking down the lane dressed from head to toe in a completely knife-club-bullet-proof suit. For a moment I was safe and happy. Then I thought of armour-piercing shells and shoulder bazookas. Not even a tank could save you from those inventions.

"Where's it going to end?"

I sighed deeply. I so much wanted to give her an answer to that terrible question.

The bungalow looked superb. As usual Mum had given it the Christmas touch. There was holly with blood-red berries behind the mirrors and clocks. We didn't have an actual tree because they were messy but Aida, Mum's friend, had brought her some evergreen ferns and these were placed all around the lounge, even on top of the television. Little snakes of tinsel glinted unexpectedly from odd places. Our little world had been transformed. I kissed Mum twice on Christmas morning and thanked her for all her efforts throughout the year.

On Christmas afternoon after a magnificent dinner and the Queen's speech, Mum and I exchanged presents. I opened mine first: a new black sweater she'd somehow secretly made,

Philip Sidney Jennings

some Irish linen handkerchiefs, two pairs of socks and a tin of shortbread from Scotland. I thanked her profusely and pushed my big parcel with the pink bows towards her. She stared at it and there wasn't a knot in her face.

"You shouldn't have done Bob. You know I don't expect anything. You're not making that much money and things are so expensive ..."

I gestured regally at the parcel.

"It seems a shame to tear the paper."

"Rip it off Mum," I said dramatically.

Slowly she unpicked the sellotape and removed the Christmas husk all in one piece. I smiled. Mum had her own way of doing things. The brown cardboard box frightened her. Her grey eyes narrowed. She went back inside herself.

"Oooh Bob."

Poor Mum. I realized she didn't know what it was. I opened the top of the box and she peered anxiously in.

"Oooh Bob."

"It's The Automatic Tea Maker," I said. "It's dead easy to work."

Perhaps it was the Christmas glass of sweet sherry that Mum had drunk that made her giggle suddenly. She picked up the tea-maker decisively.

"I'm going to try it out in the kitchen. No Bob, you sit down. I'll bring our first automatic cuppa."

My face ached with pleasure and I was just unwrapping my ninth toffee when I suddenly realized that Mum had been out of the room for something like twenty minutes. She wouldn't have gone down the lane to see her friend Aida, not on Christmas Day without telling me. A tom-tom started tapping inside me. I shot up out of my chair and rushed into the kitchen. What I saw there broke my heart and tied me up in a great bulging knot. Mum looked hurt. I saw that at once. She was holding the length of lead in her veiny hands.

The Widow's Legacy

"It, it doesn't seem to have a plug. It, it's very dusty. I'll have to give it a stripped wash."

I shook my head and spoke as calmly as I could.

"No, don't touch it Mum. I'll put it back in the box and change it."

Mum gave me a grim, piercing look.

"I'll put the kettle on," she said quietly.

I put the tea-maker back in its box and the box back in my room. I went back to the lounge and sat in front of the television. My mind was racing. The hurt inside me was so deep not even my invisible hands could reach it. Reggie, the salesman, had given me the tea-maker from the window. That I was sure of. He'd probably already sold the one I'd looked at. I wouldn't be able to change it! It occurred to me that the man's treachery had ruined my Christmas. Still I'd have to keep up appearances for Mum's sake. I smiled when she brought the tea things in and sat down. She gave me another piercing look.

"Don't be upset about the old tea-maker. We can change it."

"He gave me the dirty one from the window," I said. I just couldn't keep that fact bottled up.

"What! You didn't get it from that 'Watt and Amp' place did you?"

My head sunk onto my chest. I wanted to burst into tears.

"They're all crooks there. I could have told you that. Aida bought a radio there. She couldn't get half the stations. Blow me, then it stopped working altogether. They didn't want to change it. It's getting so you can't trust anyone ..."

Mum went on and on and slowly I regained some of my composure. I smiled and ate more toffees but the hurt was still inside me.

Philip Sidney Jennings

On Boxing Day Aida hobbled up the lane and rang on our bell. She'd brought Mum a bunch of flowers and me a little box of chocolates.

"Sit down Aida. You shouldn't have done."

"Nicest people in the lane. Wish I had a big son like you."

"I don't know what I'd do without him Aida. When you look at the world these days ..."

Aida nodded her frizzy old head. She always agreed with everything Mum said.

The television was on. Frogmen were searching a gravel pit for a missing child. I bit my lip. I couldn't take any more.

"Going to walk off my dinner, Mum."

"Yes dear. Get some exercise. I'll be all right with Aida."

I found I had walked down to the shopping plaza. Even from a distance I could see there was no tea-maker in the window. The window was full of big red SALE signs. I stopped suddenly and stepped into the newsagent's doorway. A man in a camel hair coat with a poodle on a lead had come out of the shop and was locking it up. I didn't dare move. My heart was thumping madly inside my anorak. The man passed quite close to me. I stared at his reflection in the shop window. He hadn't seen me but I'd seen him. It was Reggie.

I followed him out of the plaza. I hung back as he crossed the thin field. When he had disappeared into the wood I ran across the field and hid behind a tree. After I'd got my breath back I peered round the tree. Reggie was standing ten yards away from me. He had his back to me and was staring down at his squatting poodle. I had a long log in my hand. I ran at Reggie and brought it down on the back of his head. He fell forward into the mud. The poodle squealed. I picked it up, took it off the leash and threw the dog away. In a moment I had Reggie's leg tied up but he wasn't moving around much anyway. I looked around the little wood. There was no-one about. I knew the little wood very well.

The Widow's Legacy

Mum was still talking to Aida when I got home. I smiled at them both.

"I think that walk brought some colour to your cheeks. I expect you'd like a cuppa now."

Indeed I would. I caused something of a sensation when I opened the box of chocolates Aida had brought me.

"I brought them for you and you're giving them away."

"Bob's always been like that," Mum piped in.

I beamed with pleasure and mashed up a strawberry-filled chocolate in my mouth. Then I blinked my eyes a few times because for a moment I saw Reggie writhing in the mud and a figure standing over him.

I saw Reggie again the following evening. I was still on holiday. Mum and I were watching television. The news came on and I saw her little body tense.

"... A bizarre and macabre attack just outside Eastbourne ..."

"Ooooh Eastbourne," Mum gasped, "Well I never, not safe on your own doorstep ..."

I wanted her to shut up. I was missing details of the report.

"He is said to be in critical condition ..."

"Bring back the birch!"

As soon as those words entered the room they were picked up by the reporter:

"... Mr Reggie Jones, a popular salesman with 'Amp and Watts' was struck on the head, tied up and flogged with a birch sapling ..."

Mum was staring across the room at me. Her mouth was moving but she wasn't saying anything. I shrugged. I sounded like Mum when I said:

"Well, that 'Watts and Amps' place. He probably had it coming to him."

She nodded and stood up. She looked small and old. I wanted to throw my arms around her and protect her for ever.

Philip Sidney Jennings

She was silent.

"I didn't kill him Mum."

She found her voice:

"Thank God, for a moment, I thought you ..."

I shook my head.

"I didn't kill him. I just gave him what he deserved: a damn good birching. He knew what he was doing when he sold me that tea-maker. They can't get away with it for ever. He'll think twice in future. Any other country he'd have his hands cut off ..."

I couldn't stop myself now. I went on and on until Mum said she'd make us both a nice cuppa.

"Thanks Mum, I could do with one."

There were some girls with long legs doing high kicks on the television. Their faces were beaming and they seemed very blatant. I suddenly realized I liked looking at them but not when Mum was in the room. And where was Mum? She was a long time with the tea. I shouted out for her but there was no reply. Could she have gone down the lane to see Aida? Not without telling me I thought. I got up and wandered into the kitchen. Four big men grabbed hold of me. I struggled in the paralysis of a nightmare ...

"... anything you do say may be used in evidence against you ..."

"I want my Mum," I shrieked, "I want my Mum."

They dragged me screaming down the garden path. They dragged me past Mum, standing still as a statue in the garden. A lady policeman had her arm around her. Mum's lips moved. Her eyes were twinkling. She didn't look old and small. There was no knot in her face. In fact she looked happy as she whispered:

"Give him the birch. That'll teach him."

A Man Of Understanding

Norman Harvey

They don't exist anymore. And yet, until quite recently really, they lingered on. Small seaside towns, quietly contained as in a mellow haze of endless Edwardian afternoons. Such backwaters of passivity contrive lives of unimpassioned anguish; disquiet is fed by too-little money chasing too many doubts that gentility may be so precariously sustained. Terror lurks in the eyes of colonels pounding the promenade: death may come, in stockinged feet, with terrible stealth to the sun-lit quiet of back-bedrooms in small private hotels.

Colonel Tibbs marched briskly along the sea-front, holding himself, as always, so erect as to appear toppling backwards from a head-wind. He was a small, stringily-active man, fiercely partisan for the views of the person last spoken to. His stick, pointed towards Corunna House, swung gallantly in the bright morning sunshine. Hilda must be told and no shilly-shallying. "I am, m'dear," he would say, "only the Chairman y'know. Can't dragoon 'em, I'm afraid. You know what they are — old Admiral Freeth, Mrs. Pomeroy, the rest. Quite adamant that the place must go." The Colonel, like many shy men, spoke rather quickly to get it over with, and the tones of careful solicitude would come over with snappish acerbity; but Miss Fairchild was used to him, only the words themselves would cause misgiving.

The Council had finally voted against maintaining the exorbitant upkeep of Corunna House. The big. grey-stone Victorian house, of an ugliness so remarkable as to lend a certain interest of incredulity, had been bequeathed by some patron dying, incommodiously, without issue. The town took its good-fortune with well-bred fortitude. Nobody knew what to do with it. There had been a niece, spoken of as quite industriously accomplished with water-colours. The niece had unthoughtfully got herself married, gone off abroad somewhere. This link with the Arts had prompted the housing of the town's Art Gallery and Museum. It was much too big, the exhibits few, and nobody went there. Except, of course, Miss Fairchild. Hilda Fairchild, unpaid Curatrix of the museum's ambiguous treasures, President and Secretary and most dauntingly prolific of the Quayle St. Mary Art Society. And with whom the Colonel conducted, or was conducted by, what Mrs. Pomeroy's enigmatic daily spoke of, eyes narrowed through cigarette-smoke, as an understanding.

The understanding was an affinity of mutually-misunderstood persuasions. Setting her cap at Clive Tibbs would never occur to Miss Fairchild, but she couldn't help colouring prettily, twisting her pearls, if the Colonel trumpeted his rat-a-tat gallantries in public. As for the Colonel - well, pretty moderately fond of Hilda; a pleasantly undemanding girl of good-breeding. (Miss Fairchild admitted, untruthfully, to fifty-one, but a reassuringly powerful laugh struck the Colonel as youthfully hoydenish). His blue eyes swimming a little after a third brandy, he sometimes thought that one day — well, quite soon, really, why not ! they might as well think of joining forces, mounting a joint-operation. No more demanding word

A Man Of Understanding

was allowed to intrude and a variety of military expressions suggested themselves as fitting bulwark to the more uncomfortable strains of intimacy. And why not, after all ? he asked himself, draining his glass with quite boyish recklessness, and failing to click his fingers at the club-steward. It was so boring on one's own. Oh! the boredom, the never-ending boringness of one's own company. Why, there's not a joke of mine I don't already know, he told himself brilliantly. The Colonel often spoke, with quiet pride, of the pangs of boredom. Any less acceptable admission - terror of the barren years stretching ahead - remained unconfided even to his most secret thoughts.

But no such qualms caused the Colonel to stride out this morning with such masterful perturbation. Corunna House, after all, was Hilda's second home, Goodness knows what she did there all day - typed up a catalogue, perhaps, or moved, with careful thought, a lonely flint-stone from one overlarge table to another equally unencumbered. But it kept her happy, humming quietly to herself in the enormous, sun-lit rooms; kept her in touch with Culture, so sadly missed through the long years before old Mrs. Fairchild had died - choosing, so inconveniently, the day Hilda was to be speaking severely on the W.I.'s unaccountable indifference to the preRaphaelites.

So the meeting was a strained, unhappy encounter. Of quick, unconvincing darts towards blander topics; of the Colonel poking his stick at the gravelled entrance, fearful of saying the wrong thing, the very silence pregnant with miscarriage; of Hilda giving scrutiny to her nails, hardly knitting her brows at all, before changing the subject to touch bravely upon the comicalities of the woman who did her hair. But what, she asked, had the Council in mind. "Well, that's the rub," the Colonel seized eagerly on practicalities, "it's to be leased to some Trust - they'll be making it an Old Soldiers'

Home. See my position," he went on quickly, "could hardly object, m'dear."

So the Council was felt to have come out rather well the way things had turned out. A mere leasing allayed any alarming thought of the house failing into more dubious hands. Thus reprieved, Mrs. Pomeroy became quite skittish with old Admiral Freeth. "Oh! Admiral," she pouted, "you most unadmirable man. One was so looking forward to Saturday nights at the Bingo Hail — or even," she went on archly, wildly over-playing her hand, "what about a betting shop thing?" She smiled creamily, appreciative of the born actress she knew herself to be, while the Admiral hurrumphed in manly indulgence of Maud Pomeroy's amusing little whimsies. The Admiral took to himself a good deal of the kudos for this most satisfactory arrangement. Much to the chagrin of Colonel Tibbs. Getting positively condescending, he thought testily. Something rather offensively pointed about "Senior Service gets things done, y'know," and the like. The Colonel sniffed and walked himself, energetically furious, to a stand-still. And sparks flew from the Colonel's well-polished shoes, his stick swung in the sunshine with even more winking vivacity, as he covered the promenade on ever-more punishing route-marches of its glittering length.

Upon which was born the wheeze. Quite a good wheeze, the Colonel couldn't help thinking with the quiet satisfaction of one who often applauded resourcefulness without officiously seeking to indulge it. "A rather good wheeze," he could drop to Hilda, rehearsing casual perspicacity, "just came to me, y'know." No kind of architect sort of chap, of course, but the Colonel shrewdly observed that Corunna House was a distinctly odd shape. Bit of this and a bit of that, he mused, allowing fervour to extend to the technicalities. That sticking-out bit at the side, now - the Colonel felt sure that this eccentric adjunct

A Man Of Understanding

could be conveniently sealed-off. Even with its own side-door. Both the town and Hilda might be well satisfied. Final arrangements were yet to be made; there seemed no reason why the wheeze should not be a happy compromise.

And so it proved. The Colonel allowed himself a wary little chuckle, like a small boy surprised at getting away with something. The next Council meeting was a somnolent affair. its members comfortably unbuttoned from the quite tolerable luncheon the Clarence could put up. Eyes drooped, heads sunk lower and lower, and the Colonel's throw-away intervention, the slight, hardly-worth-mentioning variation went through. as you might say. on the nod.

And the Council acted with commendable speed. In no time at all, well within the successive Leap Years that always came upon Miss Fairchild with an odd feeling of suppressed agitation, the proposal was fact. Miss Fairchild became quite overwhelmed, Corunna House buzzing so with activity. Any number of townsfolk, drawn to inspection of all that was going on rounded off an afternoon's unusual diversion by a quick peep into the Gallery - though some, it appeared, misled by anxiety in seeking the nearest public convenience. Mrs. Pomeroy was heard to give quite unguarded approval; the old soldiers she found too sweet for words and was much drawn to a specially-designed uniform, that Quayle St. Mary might be known for its own colourful species of Chelsea-like Pensioner. Major Perryman the Warden (of many sunken ports, as the Admiral amusingly remarked) was most agreeably inclined and she found him a quite discerning man of go-ahead, yet gentlemanly, instincts.

Meanwhile, the understanding had not flowered. Neither had it withered. It stood where it had always stood. Neither flagging nor enlivened by any too-impetuously tossed bonnets over wind-mills. Hilda did have nowadays, the Colonel thought, always a slight air of distraction, quite flushed even, from all the activity. Why, he had called in at least once to find a couple of perfect strangers peering about, monopolising the place. Quite at least disturbing, that fellow Perryman forever strolling in. Scarcely an occasion now, it seemed, that that chap was not engaging Hilda with the assuming manner that the Colonel felt to be not quite the thing.

So the Colonel was seen, nowadays, on more and more furious onslaughts of the promenade. The swing of his stick had a new, savage ferocity. Hilda made too much of the chap. She was so touchingly innocent. "Howard says this... Howard thinks that," becomingly pink, all with quite unnecessary enthusiasm, the Colonel mused huffily. Colonel Tibbs had looked the chap up. Found, to his intense delight — why, a base-bound type! Could've bet on it, he told himself happily. A quarters-and-rations fellah ! He had never spoken much of his own career, but got to throwing in the odd recollection of his days with Wingate — the merest aside — an exploit here. a mission accomplished there. "What about you, Perryman ?" the Colonel demanded, "ever run across Orde at all?" Major Perryman didn't think that he had — or had he? Paths might have crossed at RMC perhaps "Fine chap," the Colonel snapped, "course I owe Orde a lot. Put me up for m'Cross, y'know. Just luck, of course," he added, disclaiming anything remarkable. Major Perryman seemed unusually silent, stood tall, passed a hand slowly over smoothly-glossy hair, turning to Hilda with some talk about next month's Flower Show.

Yes, it was all most disturbing. Something was changing — the Colonel couldn't quite put a finger on it. Something very unsettling, not quite fitting. He sat in a corner of the club, riffling his *Times,* sipping a solitary brandy with vague unease. And talk of the Devil! that chap just strolled in. Chap always looks as if he's purring ;like some sleek cat at the cream. The

A Man Of Understanding

Colonel folded his paper, made an unobtrusive exit, down the steps and across to the esplanade. Well, the chap looked set up for a while. Perhaps Hilda could spare an uninterrupted moment. Colonel Tibbs struck out, at the full-speed-ahead of expectant dismay, for Corunna House.

He walked into the Gallery and - ah! yes, there she was, seated alone, in a pool of dusty sunshine. There was something - something, really, awfully pretty about Hilda, he couldn't help thinking, almost taken aback.

"Why, Clive," she smiled happily, "hello! Splendid morning, don't you think. I was just..." The Colonel hardly heard her words. He had a curious stunned feeling, a confusing sense of being out of depth; like suddenly coming across some old acquaintance, not seen for years, caught embarrassingly in some humiliating posture. He looked stern, said quickly, "My dear, ever thought ... ever ?" he seemed to be straggling off, as if lost over some long-rehearsed but difficult message "... ever thought, m'dear, I wonder... ah! what d'you think, now... should we have a stab at... ah! well wedlock..." the Colonel stopped abruptly, as if in astonishment.

Hilda looked back at the Colonel. Her eyes strangely excited, yet with a look almost of momentary panic. "Well, Clive," she said slowly, "— what can one say? Clive, my dear," she went on, as if gathering resolution, "we're such old friends - how can one put it ? Clive, I was just saying - ah, yes to the same words from Howard. Clive, my dear..." The Colonel made a small, helpless movement. Said, "Yes, of course, m'dear ... ah, every happiness... and so on, y'know..." He turned smartly and the crunch of gravel came back into the sunlit emptiness of the Gallery.

Colonel Tibbs stepped out along the sea-front, swinging along to brave music and colours flying. The Colonel hummed lightly to himself; his stick performed a small twinkling arc, catching the sunshine. He saw far below, as if for the first time, the waves frothing in with impotent fury, claw back, recede, as if backing from the screams of a gull skimming the water-line, gathering strength for renewed onslaught.

Ah! well, Perryman really a quite decent enough sort of chap. Wonder if I'll go to the wedding? Why, yes of course. Pleased to go. Might even be asked to be best man. Best man! — ah! better man, anyway. The Colonel gave out a little barking laugh, pleased with himself. His little joke had set him up. He marched along gaily, spry, frisky almost; facing the sunshine with audacious calm. his stick flashing command, with defiance, with hardly a hint of desperation.

The Chiropodist

Ivy Bannister

'For better, for worse.' On the day that I married Hannah, I took the priest's words seriously, so seriously that four years, thirty-seven days, ten hours and twenty-three minutes passed before I forgot them in a moment of impetuousness. I was fifty-three years old on the day that I married Hannah, and she was twenty. I went into the arrangement in perfect good faith, without intimation of the sulphurous pit that lay ahead. But before I plunge into the smoke and stench of that tempestuous day, I must first illuminate the remarkable beginnings of my romance.

Oh, the foot, the foot! Its complexities are so commonly misunderstood. How taken for granted each one of its twenty-six bones is, that is, until something goes wrong!

Anyway. Believe me when I say that my snail's progress to the altar was no slur upon my masculinity. *Au contraire*, I was always in complete possession of the appropriate quantities of testosterone, and the hairs on my body sprouted in full profusion at the normal locations with particular abundance on my scalp. But before I met Hannah, there'd been no reason to rock my boat. For I was one of the fortunate few who had found complete happiness in work. Hannah opened my eyes to other possibilities. Yes, Hannah made me aware that there was more to life than attending to the eruptions and malformations that presented in my clinic.

My dear, dearest Hannah. How that young woman changed my life! I understand that there are gossips who found the December-May aspect of our relationship comical; not to mention other begrudgers who sneered because our marriage was celebrated before the grass had grown upon Mother's grave. As if I were a drowning man grasping at a straw! You and I know this to be nonsense. You and I know that the truth is simple: that I married because I fell in love. To be precise, I fell in love with Hannah's feet, then worked my way up from there.

The child arrived at my clinic one rainy afternoon with a minor complaint. Not that it was minor to her. Her face was white with pain. *Pauvre enfant*! She just couldn't tolerate suffering - or even inconvenience - in any way. When she limped into my rooms, real tears glowed in the corner of her eyes. At first I was unmoved. I listened with my customary indifference to the sound that I'd heard so many times before: the swish of tights being removed behind the screen. I certainly didn't expect what emerged. Her exquisite feet! So perfectly proportioned! Such pearly skin and the straightest of toes! All my years of experience and reserve crumbled in an instant. I stared helplessly, bewitched, unable to accept that these models of perfection might be flawed in any way. She rescued me - sweet stranger - by leading my melting fingers to the tiniest of corns on her dainty baby toe. As in a dream, I heard myself suck in my breath, then with one deft stroke, I turned the horny offender into a memory. She sighed with pleasure.

Hers was a languid little sigh that lingered in my ears. I

became acutely conscious of my telltale reactions - the stirrings of mind and body that measured the enormity of my feelings. How astonished I was! For in the past, only the abnormal foot had thoroughly engaged my enthusiasms and exercised my ingenuity. Now, my faculties were aroused completely, and all for feet devoid of ills to succour or soothe!

"You have the hand of God," she said softly. "My tears have quite evaporated."

The tears! Her tears that I had so callously ignored. Mea culpa!

But still I could not look up. I could not tear my eyes away from her sole, which yet nestled in my palm. So loth was I to abandon its bald smoothness that I invented unnecessary tasks, probing the moist dark recesses between her toes, letting my hands creep up the creamy flesh towards the ankle bone, where I sought her pulse. Pressing the palps of my fingers against that pristine skin, I measured the rhythmic pulses of her heartbeat, as if my life too depended upon them. To my surprise, my questing fingers detected an increase in pace. Could it be? Was it possible that her heart too was quickening at our proximity? Impulsively, my hands ran up her calves, where they began to massage, ever so tenderly.

She sighed again, more fully, more expectantly, and then! more demandingly! forcing me to look up. She was looking directly at me! How they dazzled me, those eyes, her eager eyes.

"You know how to take the pain away," she murmured. "Yes, in this difficult brutal world of ours, you understand how to make a girl feel good."

Her words made me shudder with delight. For it was true. It pleased me to serve. Accustomed to caring for women, I was thrilled that Hannah had recognised this in me. I felt at once the clarity of the understanding between us, smashing down the barrier of years. As I had examined her foot, she had looked into my soul. And what more could love be, than such a frank exchange? Yes, from that moment in time, I was prepared to look after Hannah forever. In no way would I stint.

"*Je t'aime,*" I said to Hannah. I was in love. And like any honourable man in love, I proposed marriage, then and there. Fortunately, as luck - and my profession - would have it, I was already on bended knee.

I have always been grateful for Mother's rearing me to be a gentleman. From my first wobbling steps, she immersed me in the requisite attitudes and manners. She taught me what was right. She saw to it that I had the necessary education and respect for authority. And she encouraged me when I decided to go into chiropody. Chiropody! Such a noble profession! The profession *par excellence* for the gentlemanly man, demanding the utmost of intellect and compassion. The hideous conditions that I am called upon to ameliorate! The blistering effusions, warped nails and ostler's toes! People respect me the way that they would a doctor, but, the joy of it is, that my life remains my own. For the chiropodist there are no peremptory summonses at any hour of the day or night. From the time I began to practise, I formed the habit of scheduling appointments around the heart of the day, just so I might stroll home and prepare a meal. *Repas de deux*, that's what I called cooking for Mother, a small joke at the expense of the ballet, if you follow me. And I never cooked beans on toast either, but a gourmet meal, salmon poached with dill, or breast of chicken and apricots.

Yes, I am very fond of cooking, French *cuisine*, by inclination. A gentleman's skills must be various. I am proud to say that these very hands of mine, which are so capable when it comes

The Chiropodist

to verrucas and bunions, are equally useful in the kitchen. I can bone a chicken and peel onions with the best of them. Indeed, I whipped up my own wedding cake myself, sculpting the icing into a frilly fantasy with sugar mice peeping over the edge of the top tier.

Like any ordinary man, I regarded procreation as the *raison d'être* of marriage. I wanted nothing more than a tribe of children scampering about our happy home on their tiny pink feet. But in spite of my best efforts, nothing happened. I didn't lose heart, for I felt confident that our difficulty would be resolved. If my experience was limited, my reading was not, and I deduced that the power to rectify matters might rest in my own hands. Since I was no longer young, I set about a sustained course of action to improve my potency. I wore loose trousers, took cold baths and initiated a regime of abstinence punctuated by vigorous coupling at optimum times.

Additionally, I made a thorough study of the technical art of foreplay, subscribing to the principle that an aroused female is a receptive one. What unexpected pleasures I discovered in the practice of this principle! I took her little feet into my hands and I kissed them. I sucked each toe in turn, letting my tongue play along the delicious nail grooves, as I contemplated the little angels that we would engender. Inch by inch, I feathered my way up into her body, until she was ready to dissolve in a sea of satisfaction.

In fact, I pleasured her so thoroughly that, one evening, she fainted. Yes, without warning, at the very height of intimacy, Hannah went limp and slithered right out of the bed onto the floor. Were it not for my presence of mind, she would have banged her head. Poor Hannah! She looked so helpless, stretched out naked and insensible on the floor. I fanned her frantically. She groaned. I rubbed her wrists, their slender veins looking too blue against the alabaster of her skin. At last, thankfully, her eyelids fluttered open.

"Dearest Albert," she whispered, "have I frightened you?"

Mutely, I shook my head, but my heart was thudding.

Her eyes latched onto mine. With a tentative finger, she stroked the floorboards upon which she lay. "Life is so hard," she said. "Desperately hard. And I am so terribly tired."

Guiltily, I propped her head upon a pillow and covered her girlish body with a quilt. I blamed my acrobatics for her loss of consciousness. However, in the very act of making her comfortable, a thought wormed into my mind: that the root of our infertility might be lurking inside her young bones.

I banished the idea at once, but from that moment on, I believe that I eyed my wife differently. I started to notice her tiny frailties, a lingering cough here, a touch of breathlessness there. Concerned, I suggested that she quit her job in the children's nursery, 'to make conception more probable,' I argued plausibly, grateful for her ready consent. I began bringing her breakfast in bed, determined to give her every creature comfort that she deserved. And the first time that I saw her stagger beneath the weight of a basket of washing, I took to hanging the clothes out on the line myself.

It was no trouble to me really. I'd always helped Mother round the house, and managed perfectly well after Mother was gone. I wasn't afraid of scrubbing a few floors. Besides, Hannah's smile was reward in itself. 'You're too good to me,' she'd say, and then laugh in her charming musical way.

But no matter how much housework I did, nothing seemed to staunch the flow of my darling's decline. Bit by bit, her gait grew more uncertain. The tears welled in my eyes, as I watched her pitiful struggle from kitchen to dining room, clutching at the walls to support herself.

The Chiropodist

I bought her a walking stick. "Albert," she smiled, "you are the best man that a woman could want. If only these naughty feet of mine would bear my weight reliably."

I took them in my hand - her exquisite feet - and marvelled that Fate could play so cruel a trick. How I longed to heal them! To paint them with therapeutic tincture! To strengthen them with poultice or ointment! But so long as they betrayed no tangible mark of their disorder, what corrective procedure could a conscientious practitioner undertake? How frustrated I was! Yet I confess: part of me rejoiced that the little feet remained unmarked. How much worse it would be if her growing disability caused them to twist or contort, to become mere grotesque appendages?

I encouraged my darling to pass more hours in bed. I collected books and chocolates and armfuls of flowers to console her. I took on the shopping and the ironing and the washing up; in short, I became responsible for all the little domestic tasks that need doing in a happy home. Eventually, when she could barely stand unaided, I purchased a wheelchair, and helped her to totter the few steps from bed to chair, where I tucked a lap rug around her knees to prevent her taking a chill.

I continued to undertake particular care of her feet, scooping out the debris from the nails, the toe-jam as we'd called it in boarding school. I buffed and massaged, stimulating her circulation to compensate for her stationary life. But as affectionate as my attentions remained, my hands strayed no more towards the regions closer to her heart. Somehow, it no longer seemed appropriate.

She didn't seem to mind.

I was often fatigued between the demands of my practice and caring for Hannah, but I never complained. I genuinely felt no inclination to protest. My poor little Hannah, *mon pauvre enfant*! How I pitied her, revolving between bed and wheelchair, and wheelchair and bed!

If only I'd been a bad man instead of a good man! If only I'd been less of a gentleman, the tragedy need never have occurred!

For I want you to know (on the understanding that you won't tell) that my beloved became something of a tyrant. "There's dust on those books," she'd shout. And I'd dust as if my life depended upon it.

"And look at the state of those floorboards. A blind man would know they need waxing!" So I'd buy wax and apply myself until my knees and shoulders ached, while she'd tap that floor with her walking stick, urging me always towards more efficient endeavours. I accepted her instructions as though they were the word of God. You see, I recognised how much she enjoyed acting my superior, and I encouraged it. Why begrudge small pleasures, where so many of the normal satisfactions of life were denied?

I should have abused her! I might so easily have found other feet to console myself with. Why didn't I? When I think of it! I could have used my clinic as a cover for the most systematic carry-on! All those helpless women, you know, feet bared, queuing up for comfort. The services that I might have provided! If only I had, then the steam that ultimately exploded would surely have dissipated in the wind, long before that terrible morning arrived.

It began like any other morning. I helped Hannah into the bath. I sat in the steam, reading out loud to her.

Dear God! I remember it as if it were yesterday! The smell of the bath oil, and me drying the nape of her sweet neck, patting gently with a fluffy towel. That alabaster skin! I

The Chiropodist

selected a lace nightgown that didn't disguise the womanly contours of her body. I kissed her good-bye then left for work. By the time that I arrived at my clinic, what had been a grumbling in my stomach had become a persistent ache; so I decided to cancel my appointments and return home for the day.

I heard the music as I turned my key in the door. The galloping strains of *Petrouchka!* I smiled, pleased that Hannah should be listening to fine music. I even paused in the hallway for a moment, letting the ravishing cadences wash over me. Already I was feeling better.

Then I noticed her wheelchair. It was empty. My heart quickened. Swiftly, I flung open the door to the sitting room. The music was loud, so loud that she didn't hear me. But I believe that she wouldn't have heard me anyway, for she was lost, quite lost, in her ... yes, in her *dance*! Oh, the treachery of her duplicity! Hair floating through air, she leapt from the table in a dazzling display of sure-footedness. Lithe as a cat, she skimmed across the floor - those very floorboards made to gleam by my own hands! The frothy nightgown fluttered over her fluid limbs, as she kicked and gambolled. Unseen, I watched her eyes, misted with a bliss that had nothing to do with me.

I clubbed her to death. No! That's untrue; I've told you a lie, for which I apologise. The case has been stated too dramatically. The very words - 'clubbed her to death' - imply a brutality of the most grotesque nature, a brutality of which a gentlemanly man is incapable.

In fact I only hit her once, and that, a clean blow to the back of the head which dropped her like a stone. Dearest Hannah! She never knew that I'd found her out. Thanks to me, she remained safe in her fantasy world until the end. In court, I listened with some satisfaction as an expert explained how that single blow had pushed her brain into the bottom of her skull.

I used the footrest off her wheelchair.

There was almost no blood, not from the death wound anyway. At once I was calm, my rage spent by that one decisive stroke. With gentle hands, I turned her onto her back, so that I might attend to her feet. She looked much as usual, with only the slightest trickle drizzling from her nose.

I went about my business methodically. *Quels pieds jolis*! I can picture them still, exactly as they were, those exquisite feet that changed my life. Yes, I did everything that it was possible to do to those feet, short of amputation. In court, they spent two hours detailing the extensive injuries, circulating a dozen photographs. They even displayed ten glass jars, each one containing a perfect toenail suspended in preservative, the ten toenails that I had excised that day with my customary precision. 'Premeditated,' they said, again and again punctuating every piece of evidence with that gloomy word. 'Premeditated.'

To tell you the truth, they said some very nasty things about me indeed.

I neither challenged the prosecution's case, nor hinted at mitigating circumstances. It would have been churlish to tell them the real story, a story that necessarily would have cast my Hannah in a disagreeable light. No, they heard nothing from me about the liar and cheat that she was.

Mon dieu! I weep great tears when I think about it. And I had always imagined that Mother would have liked her!

In retrospect I realise how poorly Hannah and I understood one another. What a strange thing human relationships are! How very peculiar the ordinary man finds them!

I got life. Yes, the jury convicted me, and the judge gave me life.

It is just as well that Mother didn't live to see me in my cell.

The Chiropodist

Her only son! But no gentleman grudges paying the price, for I did do wrong, even though the aberration was momentary.

I do miss my clinic. Happily, my memory is good, and I can bring it all to mind, all the other less exquisite feet with which I might have fallen in love. So many possibilities that might have led elsewhere! Sublime speculation! It is a most involving pastime.

Wilson Fuchs

John Murray

Wilson Fuchs was suddenly thrown out of Sanker Lee Vermin Club after an extraordinary meeting of the Vermin Committee. Two years later the authorities expelled him from the dismal annexe of the Grammar School at Gotter, though this time it was all done very properly in terms of his probationary and therefore temporary contract. In icy retrospect, Fuchs was forced to admit that that was all the job security he'd ever possessed. So, when he finally got an exacting new post in the woodwork department of a crumbling tenement secondary down in Manchester's Moss Side, he took home the densely-printed document and studied it minutely for a good two hours. This one emphatically was permanent; indeed they'd all but begged him to embrace the uniquely challenging post. Wilson Fuchs was just the man they needed. Six-foot-six, fierce, frank, immoderately psychopathic, and with a normal speaking voice which assumed the audience was dead as well as deaf. Just the man to quell a riot or a lynching, or to pick up four twelve year-old Rastas by their dreadlocks and urge them to get on with their dictations on the *spokeshave...* or Fuchs would take them all apart.

Wilson Fuchs

"The-best-are-made-of-boxwood," bawled Wilson Fuchs, once a year, every year in Moss Side. "Others-are-made-of-beech-or-ash."

Fuchs dictated with his eyes shut, in a fractured but forceful rhythm which made him sound like a drunken crooner or a muezzin. Winston Crombie, aged fifteen, had once succeeded in flinging a piece of used and bloody Elastoplast right into that open mouth, but Fuchs had responded by getting him down on the varnished floor and pouting nearly twenty ccs of undiluted Quink past the struggling lips of Winston.

Fuchs was a most lucid teacher, he had a way of really putting things across. He put little Mingus across his knee and paddled his trousers with a thick piece of warped dowelling after Mingus had called him a 'wall-eyed and hoss-faced big whore.' He made the giant of 5R, Rat Twentyman, weep with hysterical fright after assembling him for a mock crucifixion (two whopping planks of durable pitch pine) having threatened to turn him into a Messiah every week for the whole of 1982.

"I wouldn't have done it, yer greet halfwit," consoled Fuchs, squeezing the big boy gently, and lending him his bright red handkerchief. "But yer have to learn to stop mouthing off, and remember I'm the only legal boss in here."

So it went. But Wilson Fuchs did not wish to reside in backstreet Manchester, Fuchs was a countryman born and raised. His widowed mother lived in Sanker Lee on the North Lancashire coast, and Fuchs himself had a small terraced house half way between there and Gotter, Cumbria, down at Estuary Row. He lodged the weekdays in a noisy depressing bedsit in Whalley Range, but every weekend and holiday he was up there with his Lakeland Terriers, his guns and his snares and his boat, drinking his fill of one of the most beautiful estuaries in Britain. Number 3 Estuary Row looked out onto three solid miles of glittering, silver sand, curving round Greydyke in the north down to the nature reserve at the edge of Gotter Bridge. The nature reserve was famous for its unique maritime habitat - the favourite of natterjack toads. The rest of the heathland surrounding the reserve was fair game, it belonged to everyone and no one, and so Fuchs tore around blasting rabbits and foxes, he gave short shrift to the estuary's populous vermin. Sometimes too he spotted members of the treacherous Vermin Club and would take ambiguous pot shots right behind their stooping forms. Of course he was only firing into the air, or in the direction of the hills, but it had its notable effect ...

Fuchs liked going out with Herbie Leacock who lived at Number 4 and invariably told embarrassed passers-by that this was his very best friend. Herbie accepted Fuchs's ferocious generosity in the way of boat trips and loans of expensive tackle but later told the same folk that really he couldn't stand 'Bela Lugosi's big brother'. Herbie was a pale-skinned shoe shop manager and his exophthalmic wife Madgie had an identical job across at Gotter. During the week, plump Madgie fed Fuchs's Lakeland Terriers which he kept in a pen beside the allotments, wrinkling up her pudgy small nose at the stench of their special sloppy feed. Herbie and Madgie were both over thirty and had no family, but they owned a swaggering Airedale called Geoffrey and spoiled him like a favourite little son. Fuchs, frustrated through the week in Whalley Range, was always begging Leacock's company at weekends to go out shooting or trawling the bay. Herbie usually accepted with a sigh of solemn condescension but when he wasn't in the mood virtually slammed the door in Wilson's face. Fuchs would grow subdued, then stiff, then emotional, and then with a sudden confirmation of something from his distant past, would bawl to his girlfriend Sarah, standing some six inches away: "Herbie's like everyone else in this bastard Row, Sarah Stones! No constancy, no brains, no sense of humour, no *consistency* at all."

It was surprising to learn that Fuchs had a steady girlfriend and had once had a steady wife. Now forty-three, he'd been divorced since 1969 and had been with Sarah Stones since 1976. Sarah at thirty-five was an assertive, attractive, self-contained mother of two small boys, both of them with sharp, staring eyes. They were called William and Andrew and got on remarkably well with the mercurial craft teacher and lover of country sports. Divorced from a man who was a violent alcoholic with a roaring voice like Wilson's, it was as if Sarah had kept the outward marks of her previous husband, but had found in Fuchs someone who while odd was not dangerous, while loud and vehement was quite pliant underneath. Fuchs himself had been married at twenty-one to a factory hand called Wilma Fessick, a maniacally boisterous woman he had known since early boyhood. She had left him without notice one intensely sunny May morning and a week later he'd received a cheerful four-views postcard from Dorchester announcing she was happily settled with a pesticide salesman called Victor from Chaldon Herring. Fuchs had been devastated, half-suicidal, quite unhinged, even by his standards of aggressive defiance and sour disapprobation of a fickle world. It was then, in 1968, that he started his habit of bawling at everyone and everything, just as if it had seriously occurred to him that perhaps his misunderstood complexities, the deep subtleties of his misperceived self, needed to be broadcast as loudly as possible, all ambiguities to be resolved by the raw force of his lungs. It transpired later on that Wilma Fuchs had hated her awful surname far more than Wilson had guessed. Anyone toiling in a Sanker Lee button factory might have wearied of Hector the chargehand's puerile little puns on an unfortunate handle ('Wilma Fuchs and Wilson Fuchs? And that's raither nice for both parties, eh?'). In fact Wilma had tried to get Wilson to change it by deed poll to Fox, to anglicise himself in name at least. Wilson's father had been a Danish fisherman whose grandfather had been a German migrant from Hamburg. Adolf Fuchs had married Cissie Wilson in 1938 after two years of courtship consequent on his monthly fishing trips over to Gotter from Esjberg. He married and settled with a local woman in Furness-Lancashire (now part of Cumbria) but unfortunately for him when war broke out he was interned up in Cumberland as a risky alien with a most worrying pair of names. No matter that he was Danish to the core and knew far less German than English. Adolf's justifiable sense of outrage rubbed off on his only child who effectively had no father until 1946 when he was six. Penalised for nothing, imprisoned for a nonsense, a law abiding but pugnacious Danish fisherman could not help but transmit his anger and bewilderment to his growing English son. Fuchs who had loved his father to idolatry, would sooner have christened himself Wilson Excrement than Wilson Fox.

Sent on his way today by Leacock, Fuchs eventually decided to take Sarah out in his boat. Her two boys were playing happily on the sands on this blazing August afternoon, so he proposed that they leave them there while they sailed over to Greydyke for a pint and a sandwich in The Old Barnacle.

Sarah was already in her bright yellow swimming costume, plump and vigorous and sensitive and shapely. Fuchs disappeared to return post-haste in some new and remarkably revelatory briefs, and at once she winced and remonstrated. "Christ Almighty, Wilson Fuchs!"

"What yer on about, woman?" he chaffed her briskly, wincing absurdly as his bare toes felt the red hot pebbles.

"Those ridiculous trunks! Christ, the whole of North Lancs and South Cumbria can see everything you've got!"

Fuchs smirked and looked admiringly at his cumbrous

genitals. "So what? Isn't it bloody 1982? And anyway, what's wrong with the human body? Nothin at all, as far as I can see."

"It's incredibly embarrassing..."

Fuchs snarled a vigorously contorted leer. "Yes. I see! Shifting the goalposts, or call it one law for the ladies and another for the lads! Typical of your mad bloody gender, Mrs. Stones! Of course it's alright and dandy that your bits is bulging out all over like lumps of plaster of Paris? What I mean is a blind toad could see them's your ample little nellies under yon bikini tackle and that's your plump little backside down below, not a pair of yeller melons kissing."

Sarah crimsoned as two or three young couples energetically tuned in, piously fascinated by today's outside broadcast from Estuary Row. "Lower your stupid voice," she hissed.

"Bah!" roared Fuchs, salivating and glowering at the leering audience which immediately turned away. "Prewdery! I'm not one for pretence, Sarah, you know that. I don't hide *nothing* if I can help it!"

Confessing which, he tiptoed down the burning sand with his gigantic manhood bouncing like the pouch of a Furness marsupial. Sarah followed on with her graceful, poiseful gait, her trim and touching figure, and basking locals scratched their chins and wondered how it was that someone as gentle and quiet as Sarah was girlfriend to someone as shameless and uproarious and well nigh a lunatic in his extravagance.

Out in the little boat, half way between the shore and Greydyke, Fuchs decided to take a cooling plunge. While Sarah lay and sunbathed he leapt in noisily over the side. But soon irritated by the encumbrance of his trunks, he wriggled them off, cast them into his boat, and began bobbing up and down by the side of Daisy May like a bizarre little boy on a rubber tyre. Sarah, peering out of the side of her sun-shaded eyes, observed his fat penis dancing and swaying in the warm breeze, semi-turgid and batonlike, a histrionic conductor agonising over a poignant passage of Dvorak. She sighed yet ultimately concluded they were too far out for any observer to distinguish specific parts of the Fuchs anatomy.

"I hope," she murmured dozily, "no one can see your luscious behind from Haverigg prison, Wilse."

"Well I hope they can," answered Fuchs doughtily. "It might just give them a belly laugh, my moonin. You know," he gasped with deadly seriousness, "even the Queen Mother has one, Sarah, even she goes to the toilet and does her smelly business just like me and you."

"I think you're some kind of pervert," Sarah responded, almost asleep in the blissful heatwave.

"No, I's not," Fuchs retorted, blowing a mouthful of brine onto her lovely belly, so that she leapt up and took a vain lunge at his teasing form. "I'm not at all. I'm just honest, as opposed to hypocritical! I've got an arse and I've got a Charlie and I'm proud of them! That's my personal philosophy in a nutshell."

But someone could see the philosopher's buttocks. From the cottage, hidden by its high hedge and its position half way up the hill behind Estuary Row, Edmund de Sausmarez was staring at Fuchs's gigantic posterior through his Zeiss binoculars. Amused, he refocused, then saw the good-looking woman lying there in her skimpy yellow bikini. He thought he vaguely recognised her, but could not remember where it was: whether at Sanker Lee, Gotter, Lancaster or Preston. As for her companion, nude bathing, however discreet, always suggested the English middle classes, and there were few of those to be spotted in this part of the world. He could not place that bobbing naked man, and certainly not from the rear.

Edmund de Sausmarez succeeded in supporting himself by running a whole food and health food stall on the local markets, and had been living here in Spindrift Cottage for almost twelve months. Very early on he had discovered that his Cumbrian and Lancastrian patrons were only rarely what you might have termed indigenous locals. It was the undeniable truth that apart from a tiny handful of working class hypochondriacs, Edmund sold his wares to a classic assortment of e.g. art teachers and social studies lecturers, plus a copious stream of the young, pained and searching who went down to stay at the nearby Euro-Hindu Hermitage and naturally spurned the changeless local diet of... *hot pies.*

De Sausmarez had lived all over the globe in his forty years but had never been anywhere - even Athens and its *tyropittas* paled beside Furness-Cumbria and Lancashire - where they consumed quite so many pies. Even in the newsagents and sweetshops there was always a sign proclaiming *We serve hot pie's.* On enquiry the pies turned out to contain either 'beef' or 'pork', never cheese. De Sausmarez had once read an authoritative *New Scientist* article on exactly what went into commercial pork pies. Apparently the butchers took all the inedible, unsellable, horriblest bits of scrap, lights and offal, churned it all at fantastic speed in a huge electric mixer, injected it with commercially prepared 'marrow gravy', then stuffed the resultant poison into the pastry. Now and again, even if in lighthearted manner, de Sausmarez had tried to disclose such unpalatable dietary truths to authentic locals, those who stood politely bemused at his stall, looking hopefully to discover what it was all about, all this colourful hen feed.

One of these bemused had been Herbie Leacock at Sanker Lee; another Madgie Leacock surveying de Sausmarez's Thursday stall at Gotter. Herbie had lingered a good quarter of an hour scrutinising all the charming little plastic packets with such labels as garam masala, savory, lemon grass, asafoetida printed on them in Edmund's neat italic. He was entranced by the bright colours and the variations in seed, powder, pellet, of the herbs and spices. Herbie didn't recognise them as spices, though, he thought they were some kind of sweets. And so in all good faith he blushingly purchased a half ounce of turmeric, went and slouched in the nearby park and dipped into what he hoped would taste like the speckled sherbet of his remotely recollected childhood. He dipped, sucked, then spat it out amazed. Worse, in spitting with such violence, he tipped his little yellow packet and the turmeric went all over his work suit and stained it, oh my Christ! for ever more! He had to tear back home in his Fiesta to get himself changed, sweating all the way at his treacherous *curiosity*. Leacock was hardly to know that turmeric is sometimes used as a fabric dye for religious purposes in a distant sub-continent. Madgie Leacock had likewise gazed in bafflement at all those big packets of bulgur, maize, besan, sunflower seeds etc. before coming to rest on an unlabelled jar of yoghurt-coated peanuts. They looked like small white gobstoppers or the excrement of an exotic but sick animal, and she gazed at them frightenedly for minutes. When de Sausmarez, elegantly spruce in fawn cords, camel-coloured velvet shirt, dapper puce waistcoat, and, amazingly, a white straw hat *with a pink and white ribbon tied around it,* had asked her kindly if she'd like to try one of them gratis, she had jumped, flushed and darted on hastily to buy herself a... hot pie.

It was partly Edmund's left eye, an engaging poetic sort of cast to it, which had unnerved her, but his eccentric dress had certainly helped. Of course market stall men are allowed their sartorial gimmicks, but there was something about the extreme gentleness of manner and the very posh accent which made him seem of quite a different planet. Moreover, to put it coyly, he didn't exactly look like a ladies' man, though neither had anyone ever caught him holding hands with a man or mincingly queening or generally making a buffoon of himself as northern provincial homosexuals are classically expected to do as penance for their personalities.

Here he was then on his day off, the amiable posh pansy, standing alone in the acre grounds of Spindrift Cottage, gazing through his binoculars at the noisy children, the mongrel dogs, the couples, and the mysterious male arse. Edmund lived quite alone, about ten miles from the few friends he had locally, all of them employed in some capacity at the hermitage at Hanging Strand. Simon Wallace, an ex-accountant from Chesham, who these days preferred to be called Narasimha Devadasa, had offered to get him a job as an assistant gardener, but Edmund was determined to keep his cottage and his independence, particularly of the emotional kind.

Today exceptionally the wireless on his garden table was tuned to BBC Radio One, in line with de Sausmarez's relentless addiction to self-torture. To elaborate: anyone watching him over any stretch of time in his cottage grounds would have seen him periodically rush to the blaring radio, when with a look of sorrow and dampened anger, he would switch if off for about three minutes of clenched teeth, dour grimacing and carefully controlled intensity. After the three minutes was up, turning it back on, he would swiftly expel the tension in his breath and in doing so snort a hint of inhibited disgust. After two or three of these debilitating mimes, the fascinated onlooker would probably have deduced that this ritual happened exclusively when Simon Bates announced that the band coming up was called *Leyton Occident*.

"Leyton Occident, folks. The outstanding band with the outstandingly naughty message. For a change I don't want you to listen too carefully to the words of this one."

Quite, grunted Edmund. The band's name had been Timmy Badaines's invention. A football fan with a taste for opaque puns and an art college background which meant that he knew a few big words like 'occident', it was Timmy who sang lead, played lead guitar and was, in his own terms, remarkably talented. De Sausmarez heartily disliked pop music on the whole; whether gay, straight, funk, punk, soul or any other of the mad, monosyllabic categories. Edmund liked only jazz and classical music. Timmy Badaines with his London working class background had chaffed him lightly about all that, and had often chuckled at his lover's pretended affable tolerance of 'gay rock'. The chaffing however had been sincerely affectionate, as it had been right up to the very last minute when he'd finally averted his eyes to inform Edmund no, he was not going to migrate up there to Spindrift Cottage. Leyton Occident had been signed up for a Scandinavian tour so that no, the original plan of his permanently joining the band he occasionally sang for up there in Manchester was definitely shelved. Leyton Occident was destined to be very very big, he predicted quietly, unboastfully. There was no real way at all of avoiding imminent, huge success, and he even looked a little frightened as he said the word huge.

"Meaning the end of you know what," Edmund had sighed with a wind-blown expression, the cast in his eye waggling quite distressingly.

"Not at all, Ed," said Timmy, kissing him very lightly. "How could it be like that? Love doesn't die just like that, does it, like a match gone out. I'll still be up working regularly with musicians in Manchester. Inevitably. Where else could I stay but at Spendthrift Cottage?"

A Freudian slip which made Edmund weakly smile. And that was the very last he'd seen or heard of him, almost twelve months ago. As predicted, Leyton Occident had broken through to massive superfatted stardom. Now, if ever Edmund timidly rang the Shepherd's Bush flat, it was either an ansafone resonating with Timmy's jocular deadpan response, or an aggressive young man (without doubt his current lover) with a brusque and grating voice, one which immediately made Edmund apologetically yelp out that he'd got the wrong number.

De Sausmarez, impeccable dupe that he was, had let Timmy Badaines live off him for a full five years. Slaving away in a Chalk Farm jazz record shop like any uncomplaining pimp, he had made every penny of the income while Timmy had endured his many frustrating apprentice years. Flagrantly but always gently and tenderly unfaithful, Timmy had pursued his self-advance to the limits, and then, when the time was propitious, left his gentle slave to his own devices. Since when, not even a one line postcard! As if old Ed de Sausmarez did not exist and never had, just like Timmy's fatuous past. As if all that unearned money had been his minimum legal/ moral right. As if Timmy being about fifteen years his junior, old Ed should have demonstrated more sense, therefore naturally deserved his present stint of isolation. Here he was in the northern Eden then, living alone along the most paradisiacal coastline, comparable with Kerry or Barra or the Sporades. Here we find him selling wholefoods in The Land of Hot Pies! Simon/ Narasimha (Man Lion) down at Hanging Strand would perhaps have moved in with a lure and a nudge but Edmund decided patiently to preserve what slight durability was left of his old heart. Meanwhile with Edmund attending at the wake once an hour, Leyton Occident would moan on mournfully as if real tragedy were Timmy's soulstuff. When de Sausmarez knew that he was as shallow as the rock pools down there at Greydyke and that was what had been his star attraction in the first place.

Fuchs carried a string of fresh dabs as he and Sarah returned from Greydyke. Gingerly they tiptoed back to Number 3 as the sand felt even hotter by mid-afternoon. In doing so they suddenly encountered Mr. Buskerford of Number 5. Buskerford, a curt, round-shouldered but powerful man of about sixty, might have been allowed his cantankerous surliness on the grounds that his wife inside was presently terminally cancerous. However Fuchs had known him all his life and could never remember a time when he hadn't been the moody, resentful man of caprice.

"Mrs. Buskerford was certainly a second mother to me," he muttered with excessive mournfulness to Sarah. "When Mam was badly with nerves and Dad was still interned up in Cumberland, I used to play all the time with fat Dennis, him who farms at Gotter Bridge. Now he's another hopeless *bastard* who won't look me in the face, he's as surly a get as his owld miseryguts Dad. They both get things in their heads, little obsessions, no *constancy* or integrity. You know?"

As if to demonstrate his own admirably unselfish maturity, Fuchs boldly approached Joe Buskerford with a string of dabs.

"Something for you," Fuchs bawled, thrusting out the smelly wide-eyed fish. "I thought the missus might be glad... might be glad of a bit of me fish."

Buskerford glared at him incredulous. Disbelief aside, those obscenely tiny trunks gave him legitimate excuse for adopting a blankly unseeing expression, one symbolically concluding all further intimacy with Fuchs.

"No!" he said throatily but firmly. "She's too ill for any damn fish. My wife can hardly take a boiled egg, never mind any bloody mackerel."

Mackerel? He spoke as if it was Fuchs single-handedly had finished off her digestive tract. Then he stalked off, head bent, to his chickens and pigs at the far allotments. Fuchs flushed at the shameless coarseness of that refusal. Then he staggered off

Wilson Fuchs

himself, muttering and smiting at the high grass behind the Row with his string of malodorous dabs. En route he almost collided with old Mrs. Gorley of Number 2, a retired schoolmistress of eighty who had recently lost her husband. Jane had married late at seventy, her husband a widower of seventy-five being the same man she'd rejected in 1925 in favour of a dependent bedridden mother. Forty-five years on she'd had bold second thoughts and had taken a substantial risk. A fair twelve years of happiness had followed. Nothing was to prepare her however, inside or outside of wedlock, for the sight of Wilson Fuchs's horribly lush gonads thumping towards her beneath his hideous black briefs.

"For you, Mrs. Gorley," he roared, pushing the dabs into her arms before she could refuse. "If you don't want em, give em to Sammie Jack!" Then he snarled, pre-empting any arguments. "Don't tell me your little cat don't like dabs, he's a veggy-bloody-tarian?" He paused pityingly as he saw how his angry speech was making her thoroughly frightened. "Pah, knackers, I got things on me chest! But you take the fish, lass, and you and Sammie Jack have yersels a nice dab supper..."

At length, inside his terraced house, he slumped into his favourite settee and waited there miserably for Sarah Stones.

"Pay no heed," she urged him compassionately.

Fuchs snorted with bilious disgust. It wasn't, he shouted, just Buskerford, it was damn near everyone on the putrid rotting planet. Madgie Leacock moaning about the terrier feed; Herbie brutally slamming the door in his face today; Keller at the road end who barely spoke; even old Jane Gorley desperate to think up some excuse for turning down his fish.

"She's just become a widow," Sarah temporised. "And Mr. Keller's wife I think has breast cancer."

"Cancer!" blistered Fuchs derisively. "Death eh? Listen Sarah, the whole Row's all bloody *hypochondriacs,* all of them dyin to die. Don't you see? You know what we need along this row of seaside cottages don't you? Some young uns who aren't all busy bloody dyin. Plus," he shot out hastily, as he saw her about to reprove his nonsense, "my Dad died of it too, of cancer of the spleen. It tore me bloody up." He briefly sniffed and wiped his eyes before resuming his salivating flow. "But I didn't go around bloody growlin and scowlin at folk. Plus, that still doesn't explain why the Leacocks are such inconsistent wassaword summatorother *twats.*"

Sarah Stones really couldn't comment and fell silent. Privately she thought the pair next door were an extremely faithless pair of friends, like many more in this remote provincial comer. The kind who slyly crowed and prated when marriages such as hers, however violent and hopeless, broke up. The other factor of course was that most people she knew sincerely thought that Fuchs needed some sort of chromosome reduction or at least a course of horse tranquillisers from the veterinary at Ulverston.

Summer drew to a poignant close, yet things for Fuchs did not improve. He applied for several teaching posts, all within twenty miles of Estuary Row, and many at far lower salaries. He did not gain a single interview. He was unaware that after leaving Gotter he'd been blacklisted from ever returning to the county after six months earlier applying Moss Sideish self-defence in a fracas in which a pupil had been mildly concussed. Fuchs hadn't wittingly concussed him; insolent Karl Leatherbarrow had stumbled and fallen backwards to wallop his brains on a jackplane, just as Fuchs had bowled down on him with a brandished fist and a waving chisel.

At Estuary Row old Buskerford complained to him one weekend that his terriers made too much racket and it was distressing his sick wife. This of course was classic invention, but Fuchs immediately moved the pen, as calm and contemptuous as he could be when he wished. Madgie Leacock was idly threatening to give up feeding them too, so he had to plead and finally increase her wages by fifty per cent. Then Mrs. Keller died one grey August morning and after that Keller stopped even looking at Fuchs or anyone else noisy or brash or cheerful or strange. The widow Mrs. Gorley slipped and broke her ankle on the two mile shopping pilgrimage along the stones and sands to Sanker Lee. At the weekend Sarah went in and chatted to her, while Wilson did his best to find a willing co-huntsman. Herbie had a bad head cold (ha ha!) this weekend but Wilson Fuchs was not invited in to cheer him up. So that day he stumbled off alone and defiant around the claypit, and, amazingly, almost caught a fox. The Lakeland Terriers flushed it coming back over the field where the wild mushrooms were particularly copious and huge. That put Fuchs in a great fury of excitement. Unfortunately, without the speed of hounds, the terriers lost it quite near to Spindrift Cottage whose latest occupant Wilson had so far never met. Still, returning down the hill, disappointed but exhilarated, Fuchs smiled at the shining eyes and smiles and bursting tongues of the little dogs; all four; and wondered what sort of tyrant but Buskerford would not have loved them like his own. Their excited, vigorous yapping was purest, if not celestial music. And the thrill of the chase, what a feeling, what a drug, what a taste of the call of the wild..!

That night in renewed spirits he proposed to Sarah Stones and for the forty-eighth time she refused. She swore that she was prepared to stay his girlfriend for ever but never again would she marry. Fuchs turned as moody as a little boy and leaving their bedroom went and lay in the spare one, next door to William and Andrew. Tomorrow he was off back to Moss Side and his miserable tip at Whalley Range. To add to his desperation, outside a seedy bunch of motorbike enthusiasts had started tearing up and down in front of Estuary Row, singing and yelling and nastily blaspheming. The final straw, in anyone's estimation. Fuchs quickly lost his fabled patience. He flung open the bedroom window and roared at them all in great rage:

"Get the hell away from here, you *vermin!* There's a very sick woman up the road. If that means anything to your disgraceful bloody kind."

"Vermin?" a long-haired and helmeted man jeered back. "How can any bugger sleep with that orrible greet foghorn of thine?" And for good measure he gave Fuchs two upraised fingers, then farted and guffawed.

That settled it. Fuchs stormed downstairs, his brain intoxicated with a brilliant vengeance. It was a full moon and luckily for him he could easily see his target, the outlines of their bikes and their women and their studded jackets and their leers.

He flung open the downstairs parlour window, poked out his shotgun, then took casual aim. Not for a second did he worry about his marksmanship nor the possibility of manslaughter. There was a great crack and at once the back wheel of the cheeky youth's bike was punctured, his imaginative figure of eight turned into a skiting slither into the sand.

The party wound up at once, but for a few screams and swearings, and the sound of a woman howling with shock. Fuchs raced elatedly upstairs to behold a terrified Sarah clutching at her heart. Fuchs laughed wild-eyed and proposed to her for the forty-ninth time, down on his knees with his shotgun as he did. Sarah Stones stamped back into her bed and left him out there frozen on the landing where he stayed a full two hours in total darkness.

Wilson Fuchs

One pleasant Friday morning just before he drove off to Gotter market, Edmund de Sausmarez received a cheerful postcard of the Queen on horseback, one which he noted had been posted from Shepherd's Bush.

Hi
Up at Manchester this w/end to audition for new drummer. So I must of course pop over to see yr wee Spendthrift Cottage! Have to be back London by Sunday night but supposing I stay over yours Saturday? I'll be there mid afternoon I'd say in my new Porsche and will explain all, esp. the communication bizarrenesses! I often think about your Lancs idyll with remorse, regret etc. I shall see you, senor! T.

This 'correspondence' made de Sausmarez feel elated, then downcast, then pained, then confused, then queasily elated. Queasily stirred beyond measure at the thought of embracing an old lover; queasily depressed at the expectation of changeless caprice. The language as ever gave itself away. 'Bizarrenesses'? That was a breathtakingly insolent way of talking about absolute silence, unanswered letters, many mutedly desperate if the young pretty bastard had bothered to read between the lines. And then this teasing mention of *regret* on his card, the half-hearted juggling with Edmund's hankering affection, all this subtle insinuation of anything might happen favourable to a permanent reunion! Christ, what specious baloney! Timmy would be back down with 'Boris' in Shepherd's Bush by Sunday night and nothing more would be heard for another year, if not ten. And yet, the childish tormenting expectation and the hopelessly bitter impatience would not go away. It was a complete waste of effort trying to think about anything but Timmy, Timmy Badaines, for the next forty-eight hours.

Wilson Fuchs was similarly stirred. Madgie had rung him mid-week at Whalley Range for some advice about one of the terriers. It had a violent diarrhoea after guzzling some rabbit infected with myxomatosis. Fuchs bawled at her across the sixty miles to indicate which local vet he favoured, and then to his surprise he found old Herbie chirping away at the other end with real affability and humour. Herbie addled on Mateus Rosé was suddenly bored and wanted to talk to someone, even Bela Lugosi's bastard brother. The two best friends soon grew warm at each other's comradely chaff and before they knew it had arranged a full day's shooting on the Sunday. The Saturday was not in question as Herbie had to go to a cousin's wedding at Garstang.

"As best man," he mumbled, and added drily, "because they couldn't find anyone better. The devil's advocate is what it comes to, Wilse."

"Some poor fyooker signing his ballocks away," agreed misogynistic Fuchs. He forgot momentarily how Sarah Stones had rejected him fifty times to date. And then these two splendid rakes went on to bemoan Marriage, Domination, Domesticity and the rest. Afterwards overheated Herbie peremptorily commanded Madgie to make him a second cup of tea and to go and find him his missing fishing socks...

Come Saturday Fuchs repainted his boat and later cleaned his guns in preparation for the treat tomorrow. Then his contentment was temporarily shattered by the receipt of a franked and *posted* letter, which had come all the way from Number 5 Estuary Row. It was a formal request from Mr. Buskerford for the ground rent of his allotment; all of fifty pence as it transpired. Joe Buskerford owned all the Row's gardens by some complicated title deed going back to 1890, but always Fuchs, Jane Gorley, Keller etc. had paid the silly peppercorn rent by hand. Painfully suspicious in his bewilderment, after checking along the Row, Wilson discovered that all of them had received this ridiculous request by post.

"Good God," gasped Jane Gorley to Sarah after she'd come round to confer. "He must be in some frame of mind to send us these."

"He's a lunatic is what," sneered Fuchs to Sarah when they were back in Number 3. "To spend seventeen pence on each of his letters. Sixty eight pence to get back two bastard pounds! And look, they're posted from Sanker Lee, the warped old get must have driven up there specially to post them. Listen, I'll show him, Sarah, dyin missus or not! Christ! I wouldn't be surprised if it was *him* that gave Mrs. Buskerford psychosomatic cancer with his stupid bloody attitude..."

Teacher Wilson soon educated that misanthrope. He went up to Sanker Lee Post Office and despatched a fifty pence postal order by a special delivery which absolutely guaranteed arrival on the next working day. This special delivery cost him eleven pounds fifty pence and Fuchs blithely wrote out his cheque for twelve pounds (garden rent equivalent until 2006 A.D.) absolutely delighted with the irony of what he was doing.

Meanwhile de Sausmarez had given up his Saturday especially to wait for the arrival of the international rock star. He would have earned about sixty pounds on his Lancaster stall of a busy Saturday morning; but no matter where a national celebrity was involved.

Fuchs got out his guns and started whistling with joyous anticipation. Meanwhile Mrs. Gorley inside Number 2 gazed at her broken ankle and waited for the visit of a cousin aged 92 from Barrow-in-Furness. She turned up three hours late, by which time Mrs. Gorley was weeping, but her cousin who had cataracts did not see that. The young great-niece who had brought her assumed it was because of Jane's recent bereavement; not that it was the reality of being old and quite alone and always waiting, waiting, waiting...

Edmund de Sausmarez also waited all afternoon for Timmy Badaines. It was a fine, warm, tranquil day. Despite this he was almost white, quite sick with anticipation. He turned on his transistor out in the garden and of course every hour or so Leyton Occident sang their latest truculent or doleful hit, and now, uniquely, Edmund did not race over to switch it off. Time passed with leaden slowness. The clouds came out by about six, but Edmund hoped against all reason for the immediate arrival of his famous guest.

Meanwhile Mr. Buskerford watched his wife being violently sick for the eleventh time that day. Meanwhile Mr. Keller played with his grandchild Wayne visiting from Preston and every time Keller laughed and cried he wished his wife were also here to do the same. Meanwhile Sarah looked at Wilson Fuchs bent over his shiny guns and felt a great tenderness at his boyish happiness. All he wanted, not a lot, was a close pal and a job in the coastal area that he idolised. And her slender wavering hand in permanent wedlock.

De Sausmarez was sitting in the garden of Spindrift Cottage at nine o'clock, just as dusk was turning to dark. It was cold by now and there was even a speck of rain. The phone rang and his heart leapt. He raced to it but it was a wrong number! He barked and nearly swore at the person responsible and then apologised but too late. Then Leyton Occident came on the wireless for the twelfth time in four hours. De Sausmarez, like an actor in some dreary minimalist drama, resumed his mime of misery and motion and switching it on and off. He hoped absurdly for an explanatory telegram but vaguely believed such things no longer existed. There were only these Dataposts, Swiftairs, Express and so forth. Besides, half the town post offices were closed by Saturday lunchtime these days.

Fuchs was up and battering on the door by eight. After an incredible delay and the noisy barking of Geoffrey, Madgie eventually came out in her turquoise dressing gown. She was bleary-eyed, bulging with her exophthalmia, and as physically stirring, Fuchs thought to himself, as a slab of rations margarine.

"Where's that beggar?" he boomed cheerfully and Madgie jumped at that roar of his. She'd been busily dreaming about an international shoe conference, and her illustrious promotional role in it.

"Out!" she snapped.

"Eh?" said Fuchs in all smiling innocence. "Down his garden you mean?"

"No, out. Out out! I think he's gone shooting for the day. With Buskerford's son at Gotter Bridge."

Fuchs's mouth dropped open as they do only in films. He battered his great fist on Madgie's windowsill and Geoffrey snarled and whimpered with fear.

"You what," he yelled.

Madgie jumped again and frowned at Fuchs disdainfully.

"He promised to go out with me today!" Fuchs protested and there were mirages of tears in his eyes. "He promised me over the phone! All day today! I spent the whole damn day yesterday cleaning his rotten bloody gun."

Madgie shrugged. "I don't know anything."

Fuchs glared at her tautology and pointed vaguely all about

him. "Nobody here knows nowt... and it makes me bastard sick!"

Madgie bridled and actually bared her teeth. "And what's *that* meant to mean?"

"Nowt," muttered Fuchs apologetically. He remembered as she did that nobody but Mrs. Leacock would agree to feed his blasted dogs.

That was the Sunday morning when weary and nauseous de Sausmarez was lying insomniac in his handsome handcarved double bed. He felt awful as a connoisseur of awful feelings might be able to claim, yes, I have felt awfuller than anyone else in the world. The rock star had neither come nor cancelled his coming. No call, no card, no whistle, not an inkling. Worse than that Edmund knew he would be spending all day today waiting for the miracle of the eminent guest coming up even for a snatched hour of his whistle stop weekend.

Mrs. Buskerford passed away finally that Sunday, about an hour after Fuchs vanished off alone with his terriers. He'd spent the morning pacing up and down the sitting room of Number 3, singing a paean of hate to an imaginary Herbie Leacock. Sarah was knitting in her favourite chair and listening with a grimace to Radio One. Every hour her little boys' favourite band Leyton Occident came on and the two of them leapt up and down singing the quaint obscene words they did not understand and telling her what a wonderful singer was Timmy Badaines. Meanwhile 'Uncle Wilson' muttered away to Herbie, took him by the throat, cast him away, apostrophised his 'best friend', grilled him on the meaning of the superlative, asked him how his cousin would have felt if Herbie'd stood him up as best man yesterday and so on. Sarah left him to his therapeutic jabbering but sporadically urged him to go off hunting on his own.

Wilson Fuchs

Wilson finally took her advice. He opened up his car boot and ordered the four Lakeland Terriers to get inside. They scampered in and sat on their haunches panting like four little mannikins or dwarfs, Fuchs's funny-looking bairns. Swiftly he shut the boot on their grinning jaws. He was going to drive up to Gotter Bridge and set them on Herbie's fat throat, along with Dennis Buskerford's. Then he threw down his keys, swore, picked them up, reopened the boot and ordered his blinking children to leap out. Forswearing murder, he took them over to the claypit and the fields where the wild mushrooms were still as plentiful as in dreams. The terriers raced on, darting hither and thither, up and down the pit sides and the hillocks, sniffing victoriously and crazily, cocking their tiny ears at every third breath, their eyes as ecstatic and vigorous as six year-old Fuchs's the day the Home Office had let his Dad out of Cumbrian internment.

After about two hours the terriers flushed a fox...

"Fuck me!" bawled Fuchs with vainglorious joy. The fox clearly shuddered at his horrible roar. "After him!" he ordered his whiskery companions, his steadfast pals. "It'll be yon feller that gave us the dummy last time. After him, Jessie, Maisie, gwon! Come on Sam you slowtail! Go on man, get wallopin after the owd beast."

The fox tore off up the hillside and dye-ken-Wilson-Fuchs raced after it with bursting lungs. The terriers scampered on yapping and squawking, first a hundred yards, then a quarter of a mile behind, and with Fuchs about a hundred yards after that. This was a far cry from the sport of saddleback toffs, it was foot hunting as men with their rifles have been doing for centuries, helping out desperate farmers who have lost their lambs. Fuchs of course was no conservationist, he simply exulted in the chase. Without fleet hounds the race was almost hopeless, but a stroke of luck might trap the vermin somehow.

Fuchs loved his dogs but loathed all foxes. Why did he loathe them? Because they were *vermin*. Vermin being vermin; fit only for extinction!

The fox took the same route as before, up in the direction of secluded Spindrift Cottage. Where it was almost three o'clock and on his lawn de Sausmarez was having a late and solitary lunch. He was so bruised and despondent he was almost prepared to ring up Narasimha Devadasa and ask him if he fancied a different Lancastrian *ashrama*. The rock star of course would not arrive now, and yet if by a mad miracle he were to drive like the wind and then drive back to London likewise, they could still enjoy a tender half an hour together. Clutching at such nonsense, so Edmund kept on hoping like every trampled heart since the beginning of time...

Suddenly he heard a distant clamour, the sound of woofing dogs approaching up the slope. Then the hoarse unpleasant cry of a man shouting furiously behind. Had superstar Timmy got six Borzois nowadays, he wondered in impossible dread and excitement. Warily he got to his feet, afraid as well as annoyed. Before he could move further, he saw to his astonishment a little *fox* run in through his open gate! It paused less than an instant to examine Edmund de Sausmarez, then bolted up the slope of his sprawling grounds to vanish into the distant spinney.

"Thank God!" he said with a great relief, and a huge tension seemed to evaporate inside him at once. "Thank Christ for that at any rate."

He raced down to swiftly bolt and secure his gate. His heart was singing at the thought of the coming confrontation but no matter. Then the terrier dogs all came yapping up in a demented rage, viciously commanding Edmund to let them through, slavering and leaping horribly outside his gate.

De Sausmarez scowled at the uproar, turned his back and

walked back to his lunch. He'd walked about ten yards when he heard someone impudently shuffling with the bolt. Timmy? Could it be him at this eleventh hour?

He turned and saw a panting giant of a man, an outsize beetroot-faced monster about to enter his private gounds.

"What in *hell* d'you think you're doing?" de Sausmarez bawled in purest Fuchsian interrogation.

Bawled? Rage? It was a miracle, just like the sight of that vivid, beautiful small fox, just like a film star or a fantasy. De Sausmarez had yelled aloud in righteous anger for the first time in thirty-five years! Nor could be quite believe the strength of his lungs and the remarkable feeling of having made the nearby trees shudder with his colossal emotional power.

"Let me through," puffed Fuchs in a saccharine wheedling tone. "We need to get after yon fox. They go like the wind and if we traipse round the long way we'll be pushed to click the blasted get!"

To Edmund's amazement the purple lunatic began to fiddle with the bolt once again, his dogs in chorus urging him on.

"Get the *hell* out of here!" he roared. Moreover Leyton Occident had just come on the radio again, and as Edmund trembled and stood his ground he felt no particular urge to race across and lament that fickle superstar.

"I'm wanting to come in," Fuchs insisted with solemn pedantry. Though he was in fact rather baffled. It was not often anyone ever snarled or bawled back at Wilson Fuchs.

"You shall not, my friend!" shouted Edmund, stamping down swiftly to his gate. "Touch that bolt and let those dogs in and I'll call the police immediately. Do you hear me? *Do* you? I'll have you in court just like that. Now get away back down that hill, do you hear?"

Fuchs conceded to his yelling opponent to the extent of resorting to emphatic discussion. And so much for a day out he was also brooding dismally, for salvaging what was left of it! Instead here he was preparing to argue the laws of trespass with this very odd-looking toff who had a most unusual kind of attire.

"Is it against your precious principles?" he sneered at his usual volume. "You don't believe in killing poor little baba Reynard?"

De Sausmarez folded his arms, stuck out his chest and shouted back: "Listen to me, Mr..."

"Fuchs," said Fuchs.

"What?" said Edmund with a start.

"Fuchs," Fuchs insisted. "What's wrong with being called Fuchs? Especially if your Dad was a Dane."

"But I thought Fuchs was German," Edmund murmured cautiously, thinking this really must be a full-blown lunatic after all.

"My great-grandfather was German," Wilson explained with bitterness. "They interned me father during World War Two just cause he had a German surname. But believe you me he was a *Dane*. He was as Danish as Danish can be."

"I..."

"But that up there is *vermin,*" continued Fuchs imploringly. "It's fit for killing and that's all, Mr..."

"De Sausmarez," snapped Edmund.

"Diesel what?"

Edmund smilelessly informed him that his grandfather had once farmed in the Channel Isles. Whereupon Fuchs rather overdid the affable reciprocity and said, "And you were laughing at me and my fancy handle?"

"Well," Edmund said coolly. "It's just that your name in German means fox. So I thought you were making some kind of joke, or being sarcastic."

"Yes," Fuchs agreed blankly. "That's what it does mean in

German. But I wouldn't change it. Even my wife left me because of it, but still I wouldn't change my name to Fox. It would have denied all my Dad suffered through a lot of tyrannical damn *twats* at the War Office."

Then he leaned over the Spindrift gate and said with emotion, "You know how foxes kill chickens, Mr. de Summery? They rip off their heads like bottle tops! Sometimes just for pleasure, not just for hunger. They're cruel heartless beasts are foxes. They are! They kill little lambs as well and make a right bloody mess of them. They're vermin, sadists, bloodlovers themselves! They put us all to shame with their cruelty. You ask any genuine countryman and he'll tell you."

De Sausmarez stared at him without expression. "My opinions about blood sports are quite beside the point, Mr. Fuchs. This is my land and that's an end of it."

Fuchs, bitterly certain that the fox was sauntering through Moss Side by now, leant dolefully on the gate and then bellowed at his dogs to shush. He turned to Edmund and observed that the odd gentleman looked very tired, pale, and unbelievably sad. A particularly raucous pop song came on the wireless just then, and the look of fatigue and sadness on the very sensitive face seemed to concentrate in that squint and look in danger of instant expression. Fuchs was particularly alarmed at that, and so he attempted to smooth matters over with tact.

"Forgive me," he said with deadly gravity. "I'm sorry if I got you het up with these dogs of mine. It was the heat of the chase, that was all."

Edmund looked at Fuchs and noted that the apology was a bit mournful, a trifle theatrical. Not for a second did he realise that this was the same man whose buttocks had been on display out there in the estuary last month.

Fuchs again became dismally aware of his companionless Sunday. Desperate now to avert complete despair, he struck up a warm conversational note. "Do you like pop music, Mr. de Summery, that tune blaring on there?"

"I loathe it!" said de Sausmarez with vehemence. "And particularly that appalling stuff on now."

"Good man," swore Fuchs enthusiastically. "I recognise that bit of rubbish myself, funnily enough. William and Andrew think it's beautiful of course, but they're just a couple of brainless bairns."

"Beautiful?" murmured Edmund elegaically himself. "Oh he certainly was that."

"I like Emmy Lou Harris and Wally Whyton," Fuchs complacently boomed. "Or anything where you can enjoy the words and clap your mitts and scream a bit. Sarah says the words on that record are filth but it's meaningless nonsense to me, nothing else."

De Sausmarez stared at this garrulous, artless giant and realised that at least three quarters of the world knows less than nothing about the love of man for man. Fuchs whistling casually, then lied. "I'd better be scooting. I'm off out with my mate. I..."

Edmund observed him with a little less disgust now that he was offering to depart.

"I..." Fuchs vacillated.

"Yes?"

Fuchs burnt his boats and dived straight in. "How would you like to come out fishing in *Daisy May?*"

"What!"

"There's plaice out there clustering round the Gotter shit pipe and the taste, man, is just out of this world!"

"You..."

"Now! Go on! Now would be ideal! Come on! Plaice are

bottom-grubbers, they like raw sewage better than owt. I can't ask you out gunning, but surely you can bloody well fish? I mean Christ, even bloody vicars *fish!*"

Edmund hesitated for just two seconds. His refusal when it came was very polite, a perfect gentleman's in fact. A sensitive mannerly evasion which left Fuchs really touched and even more anxious to undo what distress he' d caused. Wilson Fuchs then made about ten different friendly offers ranging from the immediate loan of his hedge trimmer to a *family* meal this evening down at Number 3. Finally he settled on a friendly drink they would have together in Gotter in the maddeningly nebulous future. Then just as Edmund ran out of patience, Fuchs noticed Herbie Leacock's car turning in down below into Estuary Row. And thought he might just be able to persuade him out into *Daisy May* tonight, if the weather did not break.

"My best friend," he bawled as he tore off down the hill with his ecstatic little dogs. "Or at least the bugger thinks he is."

Abe Poge's Book

edited by Stephen Wade

11th. Nov. 1778.

Ye Gods! Today was the worst day of my life. Delays and tribulations pursue me like a pack of hungry curs chasing the fox. I am a hunted man and Fate is in pursuit. Does Genius ever bear such pangs? The day began ill, when I spewed mightily on rising from bed, and my pate overhung the tub for close on one hour. My good landlady, Mrs. Turtle, did wax most satirical. She did aver that filling my maw with sack and delicacies was the cause. Yet surely a man — a literary man to boot — needs the sensual gratification of a good piece of hoggery from time to time. Nothing tempts the lips more than a slice of seed cake or a joint of lamb.

Well, there I was in my nethers when Mrs. Turtle 'gins to snigger most rudely at my plight. I was owing three weeks' rent, else she would have received a bowl full of piss in her visage!

Worse was to come, for on sitting at my desk, I discovered that the papers on which I writ my epic prologue had vanished. Just imagine my plight. This was the opus that was to take my name into every literary weekly in London, and it had gone! Mrs. Turtle vowed she had not lighted the fire with them, and so a search began, and egad, if the cat had not taken them to have her messy kitlings on! That tabby whore has been with kitling for two dozen times — I swear it. The sides of Nature will not sustain it, as the Bard says.

There was the bloody sludge and the squealing things mewling most pitiably. My heart would have gone soft if 'twere not for the huge difficulty in distinguishing the letters of my masterpiece that lay besmirched beneath.

Well, the day began so ill that I took tea and coffee and some stew at Grim's House and then returned to the garret to write my resolutions. Be it known to posterity and to future scholars of my scribblings that on this day I did peruse a holy book that has fair changed my life: 'tis named, *A Grave Way To Follow To a Sacred End* by the Rev. Barebones Harm. A mighty good book in troth. I did sit at my desk and pen these resolutions, so disgusted was I with my heathen manner of existence — I cannot call it 'life' for I am unknown and may as well be a grub in meat for all the booksellers and patrons acknowledge me.

1. No more will I spit in Mrs. Turtle's Hot Pot on the way out for my dinner in the alehouse. This is vile and petty jealousy and to be abhorred.

2. I resolve not to attend bear-baitings, for several reasons, the chief being that an melange of a cur's brain did splatter my best fustian the last time.

3. The whores must be left alone. The wooing exhausts and the mating infects. At least, a better natured wench is needed, and one that does not sell her gate of Venus for a groat.

4. Leave off indulging in strong wine for it does oft lead to a carousal that deprives me of food money so hurtfully that I have very near died through lack of vitals in the courting

season.

5. Resolved: not to copy the hackwork of others as this only leads to poor reputations and squabbles in the gutter press.

6. Stop the swearing and blasphemy that ensues at dinner with Mrs. Turtle when her disgusting menagerie do excrete and vomit on my person: her invitations to dinner are to be prized in a lean week and she could send me to Newgate if she had a mind.

7. Leave off pissing out the window in thy drunken fits. 'Tis bad for the soul and in addition, does oft splash on the desk if thy aim is poor.

8. Fight the Green-eyed Goddess. To be jealous of old Ned Dirge and Lord Shortbottom merely because they are corrupt and would lie with a leper to see their name in print — this is evil and will send you to Satan. One day they shall be lower than you and wait at your levee for favours.

9. Leave off robbing children of bagatelles and sweetmeats when thy stomach rumbles and you dare not tackle a man.

10. For the Lord's sake, frequent not the theatres. The fruits of this are the pox and mayhap a knife up thy skirts.

My soul already feels better for these resolves, and to be sure, they will be kept. A great writer cannot show weaknesses of will and spirit. And yet, and yet, was ever Shakespeare cursed so by the hard irksomeness of common life?

Because of the kitlings, I have forgone my epic and now do propose to myself a long verse satire in the manner of Pope, yet better. 'Tis to be called *The Dirgiad* and will be aimed at that petty scribbler Ned Dirge who grows fat by his pen while I rot in this rat-infested den. The poem will cruelly torment in words the folly of those who live as flatterers and sycophants and who hope to gain immortal life by their pens. Lord Shortbottom and his tragic dramas of 'Ordinary Wheelwrights And Shepherds' will receive my sting. All other pretentious oafs and

Abe Poge's Book

snakes of Grub Street shall perish. Makers of sermons who never prayed once in their lives; poets who ne'er loved yet pen sonnets; historians who chronicle falsities; hacks who tell lies of the great; Dirge, who dresses the dandy and the macaroni cause of his comedies — all shall go down with my abuse. My satire has gentility and restraint however, as in this from my prologue;

> *No tale of Dirge was ever heard,*
> *til was heard the word 'turd'.*
> *This described him brain and all,*
> *Yet the nit-head had the gall*
> *To pen his plays and call them great,*
> *When bedding punks was all his fate.*
> *At the most potent Spring equinox,*
> *He woke and yelled out "Tis the pox!*

So it goes on, most good-mannered and with real spite always held in check by my breeding and natural love for all men.

To end today's notes, once more I must report failure in the druggist's shop. The wench will have none o' me. I essayed to use the bold attack today, advancing to the small closet as she rummaged there for some swelling—tincture, and she, the lithe young creature, like a young foal, whinnied and bolted when I did pinch her plump rump. Egad — 'twas a thrill and my member reared his head like a snake from a basket. I' faith, he has been wriggling in the basket too long. If young Jenny yield not soon, 'tis to the whores again, and oh, by the Divel! How I do dread the barber's liquors and heats to cure me o' the pox. I have raged for hours on end and scratched out a Russian Winter in the anger and passion of it. A man of letters needs his country pleasures — no more than a rake or a good Marquis. I will have her and be damned!

I think mayhap 'twas my plague-marks — I must powder them over and water my pate with French juices.

15th. Nov. 1778
I sit down a disappointed man this night. There are men in history who have tried to sway the development of literature. Ben Jonson and his Tribe; Petrarch and his circle; Sam Johnson in our age — these have tried and I thought to have joined them with my Projectors Club but it was not to be. Oh Achilles! The little men in this world! I had not thought Hell had undone so many. At nine I took a seat and waited, expecting some few, discerning scribblers searching out helpmates in the battle with the booksellers, but what did Abe receive? A veritable HERD of poetasters and pretentious do-ought-for-a-groat, rag-bag, slovenly hacks.

They asked after me and then proceeded to wait for me to purchase the tea and supply the pipes of baccy! The effrontery! I was assured that, "'Tis the custom when starting up clubs. Old Rigg did so when we came to join in with his Agricultural Writers Club, and that Rake Nabb did so when he trumped up his Theatre Hecklers and Hooters Club — oh yes, 'tis the custom."

I was flabbergasted and enquired whether any man had brought with him any projections for Great Works? A hundred answered and all tables were covered with scrappy scribblings. Then the worst happened. A huge and vicious fight began as to who should read from his epic first. They would have rendered a cacophony fitting for Pandemonium had I not ordered them to be silent and pointed the finger at one young man, more tough and vociferous than the rest, to read. He stood, gulped down the dregs of his tea, and said,

"My epic poem concerns the exploits of Milton, our greatest epic poet. 'Tis high time someone writ of his epic doings...."

(Cries of, "Come, render, RENDER!")
He began, in a high, whining voice, like a stuck pig;

> *Great Milton's art was well given shout*
> *When first his orbs were stricken out.*
> *The clouds dispersed, the rain ceased,*
> *And John did come and make his peace*
> *With Lady Art, his closest friend,*
> *Whose reign began when sight did end...*

"Does it go on?" I asked. He said that it lasted three hours for he had read it before when he had got his listeners drunk.

" But this club is only for talk of projected works... we aid each other to create..." I clamoured. This was my greatest error. They began again, yelling out their schemes. I had plans for verses that enumerated the Beauty of Pigs; satires on the Management of Gardens; allegories of the Gods of Tibet and fairy tales of Ancient Atlantis. One man proposed the utter abolition of words and proposed stories in actions and grunts. By ten I was wearied and escaped them in a frenzy.

My worst enemies, ye booksellers, sons of Satan and black rogues, do not often surprise me with some short show of liberality, but old Sol Slim did today provide, with some smirkiness about him, a list of his needs, and this is a boon indeed for a literary man struggling with the labours of invention. 'Tis as follows:

First and most pressingly demanded by the customers are those new stories that do delight the fairer sex. Mr. Richardson's 'Clarissa' was so welcomed that if ye can hammer together some tale of scheming seduction of a maid by some dark and cod-faced fellow, then 'twill be assured success.

I know not why these sinful and luxurious series of bedroom dramas and fox-chasing tales please, but there it is — one more instance of the folly of the masses and the decline of our literature. The list goes on:

Always welcome are sundry romances but not of the pastoral kind for the public is heartily sick of these and is like to protest. Include some delicate moments for the intercourse of young people in the softer feelings. Names have been somewhat lacking in originality of late: no more Phyllis, Damon or Arethusa — this is now vulgar.

Well, I never did like the pastoral. Plot was a difficult taskmaster and I have begun and abandoned a dozen. There was but one item on the list that appeals to my pen and fancy — and I aim to essay it — 'tis the tragic drama.

This is what the good Slim says of it;

The mob in the pits never tire of a good, passionate and historical drama. The higher they fall from the better and if a wag could set a plot on a lofty precipice, all the better for sales.

There we are, oh, Posterity! Now I find my metier. Why did I not see it before? The Muse has only this day picked me out for glory. But more — I have a plot. Like all great tragedies, it concerns true history and if authors have sung of Sophonisba and Harry Percy and Cleopatra then to be sure, Abe Poge can sing of Epaminondas. The wits will stumble o'er articulating the word, but 'tis time they were foxed. 'Twill describe our hero's rise from lowly field-keeping in Thebes to the high eminence of leading the Theban forces. He is continually pestered by critics, hampered by superior bunglers, beleaguered by politicians and misunderstood by the nearest of his blood. 'Tis much similar to my progress in the world, and my feeling for him will show through the words in which I pen him. As usual with such protagonists, he must have some physical handicap and this has to be original, therefore is plagued by the stomach cramps (again, as is his creator) and he is victorious in spite of this.

The bugbear with this species of composition is that fools

and poetasters step forward and offer prologues for the price of six pence. I myself have twenty such pieces in my drawer here ready for use, to fit any tragic subject. In truth, I have one ready writ for Epaminondas;

> *Behold the mighty once more tread the bare planks*
> *And all but villains bow to give him thanks,*
> *For he has brought back to the dying stage*
> *Noble passions, quick fits and red-cheeked rage.*
> *Great Sparta falls to his sturdy arms*
> *And all that defeats him — a lady's charms.*

One of my best is't not Posterity? Of course, a woman must bring about his end: 'tis always so with these tragic heroes. I will be subtle and call her Dooma. Thus meaning to be highly symbolic of the lady Fortune. Will the wags spot that?

Harry Curb has promised to dance, a jig 'tween the acts if I do mention his name to Lord Shortbottom.

Now, most dear journal, I report on young Jenny. By Juno, I was close on success this day. The filly was sporting with some sweetmeats and conversing with a buck on the steps of her shop as I did walk by. I tipped my hat and smiled, slyly asking if she did drop a sweet. She looked upon the earth and there I had a brief peep at her melons — 'twas rare. To squeeze them would be highest bliss. Then, to my great good fortune, the young blade walked on and I was left alone with her. She did blush and fumble with the door handle, making escape, so I took her hand on the handle and did squeeze mightily. The wench did slap me, but 'twas worth a buffeting! It is some progress, surely, to do thus? Yet, on reflection, her face did show a huge repugnance at my squeeze — I think 'tis my lace sleeves that she objects to. Her retreat was swift.

Mayhap, 'twas my new boots that did offend her, as they shine most *à la mode* and show, it could be, a dandy temperament? Egad, the girl needs an old Tory.

N.B. knock the maggots out of the meat afore they do gorge it and leave Sunday dinner bare.

Mayhap, 'twas my new periwig - a trifle too arresting?

A Small Window On Gomorra

James Waddington

My quack thinks I'm a sadist. Not so. I keep my distance from the great Marquis, in temperament as well as time. But I had to get rid of her, that particular girl.

She wanted me to look at photos of the little farm, her doltish brothers, Rose the cat. She tried to give me a present of a childhood treasure, one of those garish plastic windmills on a stick which she had bought "with me own money, at the fair, in Sligo."

There was no hard feeling on my part, no bitterness as far as one can tell on hers. She was upset, of course, but young girls cry easily, and I'm sure within a week she was running around the midden with Rose the cat and the clodhopping Michael, Seamus and the rest, laughter on her lips and only the fading shadow of a trouble in her little breast.

Or am I too pessimistic? Could there be any hope that, while she may have come in the spirit of one of the more self-mutilating saints, she should have returned with an infective splinter of enlightenment lodged in the large, but largely empty, organ of her mind?

I could consider how it might have been, how it might be -

James Waddington

not the least amusing way of passing a morning, now I am forced to rise so early. My cigars, a glass of brandy, a good fire burning; the girl's successor, fine plump Sadie with the brain of an ox, to bring me coffee when I need it and stand there saying "Will that be all, Sorh, will that be all, Sorh," but not moving when, idly with one hand beneath her skirt, I do things which make the dew glisten on her upper lip.

The other would have leapt, skin flicking, like a foal that feels the switch laid gently to its side. How did she come to change so? I could consider. Vain speculation, no more.

Three nubile adolescents are sitting in a crowded café in downtown Sligo. (Imagine downtown Sligo for yourself - I have no idea.)

The girls are dressed, so they would think, 'smart', in garments with inscriptions of which they themselves do not know the significance. If you say, "Why do you have the words Dirty Harry scrawled across your delicious little bosom?" the reply will be, "Well, sure it's after being Dirty Harry, don't you see?"

They are Kathleen, Mary and Bridget. Mary is working up to be a Bride of Christ.

"The fact remains," Bridget is saying, "London is a dreadful wicked place where they have bookshops with pictures of people doing things it would make you sick to look at and turn your hair grey in an instant, and them not taking a blind bit of notice as if it was the most natural thing in the world." One understands that there are no such bookshops in Sligo. She's probably talking about Smiths.

"What kind of things would those be?" asks Mary. Her excuse is that she must understand before she can condemn.

"Like MacAllister's bull with the great bollocks on it?" breathes Kathleen so softly that the youths at the next table

A Small Window On Gomorra

barely catch her words, yet they shift their spotty buttocks in discomfort.

"Look would you just watch the gob," says Mary, "otherwise Father Kelly'll have me in the hair shirt and ashes for another fortnight." She giggles.

"Much worse than MacCallister's bull." Bridget wants to keep the conversation serious.

"Oh tell us, tell us please," pleads Kathleen. She puts out her tongue and pants. The boys at the next table keep their eyes fixed on the red check plastic table cloth.

"Well, you know the picture books at school in the cupboard Mrs MacLaverty was always the maniac for keeping under lock and key, you know the picture with all them people with no clothes on, the one with the strange birds and the globes of glass. You know the man with the daffodil up his bum...."

"In his bottom, if you don't mind," says Mary. "Well?"

"Well!" says Bridget, and doesn't know how to go on.

"I tried it once," says Kathleen.

"You never," says Mary, staring at her with wide blue eyes and a vigorous, healthy complexion. "You're as good as telling the devil to come and get you now. What possessed you to do such a thing? What a terrible risk you would be taking with your mortal soul. Was it worth it for a few brief moments of.... What was it like?"

"Well it wouldn't be going up at all. A daffodil stalk's awful bendy."

"And what did your confessor say?"

"He said it was. He said it's a terrible bendy thing a daffodil stalk. He gave me ten 'Hail Marys' and told me to be careful in future because the juice is the terror for being alkaline."

Mary turns away, re-packing her mind neatly. She tightens the straps, and then speaks:

147

"Anyway, Bridey dear, what was the point you were making?"

"That in London it would be very easy to fall pregnant without you scarcely knowing how it happened."

"Why would a girl who is determined to keep herself unspotted be any more likely to fall pregnant in London than in Lochmaleish?"

"Because Jennifer, and Edna and Cousin Bridey and Mary Madden and Eileen, none of them fell pregnant at all in Lochmaleish, and every one of them was up the spout when they hadn't been in London six months."

"They must have fallen to temptation then."

"My point precisely. And my further point is," and Bridey waits until the other two, eyes shining and cheeks glowing, have an ear each close to her coral lips before she continues, "my further point is, the future's not ours to see, *che sera sera*, and would it not be the sensible idea if we thought about precautions now, while we have all our faculties about us."

"But it's illegal," says Mary loudly, sitting upright in her chair and drawing the glances of several of the clientele.

"Wisht girl. What I'm thinking," Bridget continued, "is this. If a girl is to fall - and she is, I'm afraid, she is - what's the least sinful way of going about it, the one that wouldn't be upsetting the Blessed Virgin too much at all?"

Mary knows that a wicked trap can be baited with an accident of virtue.

"Is that not a wee bit presumptuous, to be bringing the Holy Mother into it? Should we not be leaving the whole question to them as are qualified, and not be meddling in what doesn't concern us?"

"But," asks Bridey, "will them as are qualified be there to give us the answers when we're in the grip of the overpowering temptation? I'm sure you know what I'm talking about, don't

A Small Window On Gomorra

you Kathleen?"

"Oh I do," breathes Kathleen between parted lips, plunging her hands between her knees and rubbing the palms together.

"What is certain," continues Bridey, "is that one is always sorry after."

"A bit," sighs Kathleen.

"Are you not always sorry after, Mary?"

"After what?" Mary's blue eyes shine like mirrors. Her mouth has a sweet hard smile.

"She knows," says Bridey to Kathleen. "Look, suppose I was to fall victim to temptation in London, I'm going to be sorry. I know that. What I want is to be no more sorry than I have to. For instance, is it right I should bring a little babe into the world, conceived out of wedlock, poor and fatherless?"

"You should not!"

"Then she'd have to be taking the precautions, isn't it so?" says Kathleen.

"The precautions," says Mary emphatically, and then, after sharp 'sh's from the other two, repeating it more quietly, "the precautions is not doing it in the first place."

"Sure I know that, but that's a counsel of perfection."

"If I don't do it in the first place for much longer," says Kathleen, "I think I'll go into convulsions."

"So it's the precautions it'll have to be. And that's where you can help Mary. If you have to sin, you'd be foolish not to be going for the least wicked. Of the precautions, Mary, which would be the least wicked, would you say?"

"The Church allows the rhythm method within wedlock."

"The Church is a blithering con then," says Kathleen. "Me Aunty Elizabeth and me Uncle Mick use the rhythm method and they have the nine already and only been married twelve years."

"Now," Bridey continues soberly, "of the effective

precautions there's the two different approaches. There's the physical barrier, and there's the hormonal intervention. Now is it the truth, Mary, that once the fella has his willy up you, the most virtuous thing you can do is just let him hump away till he comes? Is that not so?"

Kathleen moans.

"You're in mortal terror of hell fire even thinking such a thing," says Mary.

"I'm only thinking about it," says Bridey, "like you'd puzzle out your homework - which I couldn't say for sure is the case with Kathleen here."

"It's mortal sin," says Mary.

"But that's my point. If it's mortal sin for him to have his willy in there in the first place, can it make it any worse for him to be having a johnny on it? And would that be more sinful than the tablets?"

"Holy Mary Mother of God, I can't be listening to this any longer. Do you think you can choose between the badness of sin? Sin's not like that."

"Have some sense, Mary girl, of course it is. What would be the point of having mortal sin and venial sin at all, what would be the point of different penances for different sins if they were all the same?"

Mary looks hot and cross.

"She's got a point," says Kathleen.

Mary tries the hard sweet smile again but the lips tremble. She frowns instead, but can think of nothing to say.

"I know it's difficult," says Bridey.

"Difficult. You're talking as if it was a horse race. Would I be better going for a winner, or would I be better putting a bit each way?"

"I think you're beginning to follow me," says Bridey. "I mean if I'm not tempted, then we're laughing, but if I'm swept off my feet, surely to God it's best I fall as soft as I can."

"I wouldn't know where to begin."

"Well let's set about it with a bit of organisation. Here's a page out of me diary. Let's write them all down, then we'll put them in order. Precautions; physical barrier. Precautions; hormonal intervention. Oh and there's the Intercourse itself, we mustn't be forgetting that."

"You can't have precautions without the intercourse," says Kathleen. "A fella would look a right dickhead sat all by himself with a johnny on his plonker, reading the newspaper."

"Could we not at least keep the language a little bit decent," says Mary.

"That's a thing," says Bridey, "are the tablets a sin until the moment of intercourse? If not, at what precise point does the sin commence? Is it with 'the introduction of the very tip of the glans between the outer lips of the vagina', is it with 'full penetration so the hairs of the pubes meet', or is it 'at the moment of ejaculation of seminal fluid into the upper reaches of the vagina, against the neck of the cervix'?"

"Will you shut your gob," says Kathleen, "or I'll be having the convulsions now. What about if he whips his cock out just before he shoots off?"

"That's the point I was making. Would that be even worse than leaving it in?"

"No, no," says Kathleen, "I mean as a precaution."

"Och, I'm with you. Precautions; physical barrier. Precautions; hormonal intervention. Precautions; if he whips his cock out just before he shoots off."

"Oh dear," says Mary, as of one who has tried and tried and of whom no more can be expected. "What else?"

"Unnatural acts," says Kathleen.

"Like French kissing?" says Mary. She can but hope.

"Like cocksucking," says Kathleen.

"Holy Mother save my soul."

"And daffodils."

"Och we'll have no time for the flower arranging," says Bridey, "but the other ought to go down. Even if it is no more enjoyable than it sounds, and wouldn't you think it would have to be, there's all sorts. What if he slips it between your tits? What if he tickles your lug with it?"

"Will you shut it?" says Kathleen, "or I'll have to be taking a short walk." And, by Jove, if the actual girl had spoken as these do now, and not tried to interest me in blurred snapshots of her cat Rose, she might not be back in Galway today. But no matter. I strike the bell. Sadie will soon be here with the coffee.

"May the good Lord preserve you and keep you from your wicked, wicked thoughts," says Mary.

"I wonder where the sin is exactly," muses Kathleen.

"Is it not obvious? I never even knew it was possible to think such thoughts, let alone say them aloud. Oh Holy Mother..."

"No, I mean the sin in the precautions. With a married couple, say a married couple with six children, where would be the harm...?"

And here we leave them to go through the fascinating conundrums of Catholic theology. After an hour or so more of attentive discussion, Bridey and Kathleen at least will have convinced themselves that there is nothing peculiarly or overwhelmingly wrong with 'the precautions'. It's a conclusion that well-adjusted catholic couples come to quite naturally after their third or fourth child, without all this ridiculous argument.

"But it's mórdher, is it not mhórdher," the young woman protested when, after the disturbed few weeks which led to her unexpected departure from Lochmaleish and, under my roof, six months of violence to everything she held sacred, she came

A Small Window On Gomorra

to me not with more photographs of farmyard chums, but the news that she hadn't had 'the chórse' for two months and felt herself to be with child. I think despite what she had been through she saw herself on a donkey, in something blue and voluminous but becoming, heading for a stable.

When I say violence, I don't of course mean anything physical; but her beliefs were badly bruised.

I talked to her. I explained how everything was, if not for the best, at least not for the worst. I wonder how it ended. Mere vanity.

The same cafe in Sligo - or another very like it.

"Was it terrible, the abortion?" said one.

"The termination. It was, indeed it was terrible, it's like losing your heart, it's like grieving waking and sleeping and not being able to grieve enough because you've lost the bits that help the grief to heal itself," - or something to that effect.

"And have you confessed?" said the third.

"I have not, not yet. I haven't the strength a while. Is it not a terrible sin?"

"It's the worst," said the third, "it's mhordher."

"So I thought. But we talked a bit, him and me, and he was ever so understanding in the way you'd never expect. Do you know what I think now? Sure the wee soul only flies away to limbo, without the faintest notion that it even exists. Now what is the soul, could you tell me?"

"Sure the soul's the spirit," said the first after a weighty pause, "it's the bit that goes on for ever when the body has returned to dust."

"Does the soul know of its own existence?"

"These are terrible hard questions you're asking," says the third.

"Does the soul exist in its own consciousness, or in the

consciousness of God?"

"How would I know?" says the third.

"Och Jesus and Mary, do you think you exist or do you not?"

The third shrugs.

"Have a guess, yes or no."

"How would you tell?"

"Are you serious? OK, forget it. Just get a hold of this. If I exist only in God's consciousness, then I'm either something like a stone, or I'm part of God - and that's contrary to the Catholic faith to say I'm part of God. And I know I'm not a stone."

"How do you know you're not a stone?" asks the first, who recognises this for a philosophical discussion but can't get the drift.

"Well, do I look like a stone?"

"You do not."

"Have some wit then. Honest to God. Where was I? The point I was working round to is, if I don't exist in my own consciousness, I don't exist at all."

"What about the stone?"

"What about it?"

"Does it exist in its own whoda?"

"Well what do you think?" The second girl is getting exasperated.

"I would think that it didn't. But it exists, all the same. Something doesn't have to exist in its own whoda to exist."

The second is entirely nonplussed. Then she sees. "But a stone is a thing. You can see it, you can touch it. It's thingy." She is struggling again, but not for long. "Take away the stone from a stone, and what have you left?"

The first shrugs. "And that," says the second, "is the condition of the soul without self-consciousness."

"Could you not put it a bit simpler," says the third, "for the distressed of brain."

"Souls in limbo do not exist. Therefore, theologically speaking, no crime has been committed. Abortion," she rose and curtsied," is not murder. Q," she conducted each letter archly, finger tip to thumb, her blue eyes shining like mirrors, her mouth in a sweet hard smile, "E, bloody D."

Old women mumbling their tired fig rolls looked horrified. The girl sat down.

"Well, in that case," said Bridey, "where will we be putting it at all in the list of sins? Wait, I have it here," and she drew out of her handbag the page of the diary, grubby now with addenda and consultation.

"It was bad was it, the termination?" asked Kathleen.

"The worst."

"Worse than unnatural practices?"

"Much worse."

"Its own punishment, could you say?" asked Bridey, pen ready.

"You could."

"Then if the wee soul comes to no harm, it's hardly a sin would you think." She put the list back in her bag and dropped the pen in after it. "I don't think we'll even be bothering to write it down at all."

"Are you truly sorry?" asked Father Kelly through the grille.

"Oh I am, I am."

"Sure you were always a good girl. We sent you into the world for a space because we detected a questioning spirit. Satan found you out, Satan made you fall, but perhaps it was God's will. You have no doubts now, do you child?"

"None, Father."

"I knew you would come back, my child. Before, you were

not ready to leave the world, but I detect a change in you, a new certainty. Do not let it go too long. Come to us when Jesus calls you. How do you think you will serve, my child? In the world, with care and sacrifice, or will you leave the world for a life of prayer?"

"In all humility, it was the study of theology I had in mind, Father."

Vanity, mere vanity, but ... bitter in years, I still have hope.

Any Old Fart In A Storm

Elizabeth Howkins

On the day that Milton was declared brain-dead, seven unattached females of a certain age shot craps for his body outside the I.C.U. Gerda was nervous as she blew on the dice, sending a wad of sugarless gum pirouetting through the morning air, redolent with room-freshener and pee. The faint moustache above her lip quivered in annoyance. She felt that her claim was paramount and viewed her participation in this tasteless, Runyonesque competition with barely harnessed disdain.

She needed a date for her thirtieth high school reunion. The situation was critical. You can't just rent a date like you rent a bike, she thought, unless you want a gigolo with pointed shoes and a waxed moustache. Having been voted the senior most likely to succeed, it was unthinkable for her to attend the gala if she could not even succeed in getting a date.

Hilary, on the other hand, felt that her claim was stronger. After all, hadn't she graciously, if reluctantly, given up a septuagenarian with a steel plate in his head and a quadruple bypass in his chest, handing him over to her friend Louise who was terminally ill with an exotic skin disease that caused her to shed her epidermis bi-monthly in five inch sheets. Louise had made it clear that she felt that her impending death gave her a pressing claim for male companionship. Hilary wasn't sure about the validity of this argument, but she stepped aside gracefully when Louise threatened to blow her head off as she had nothing to lose. Hilary had also felt that her failure to defer to the terminally-ill might be viewed as petty or mean-spirited in some circles and, basically, she was a compulsive pleaser.

Mia also felt that her claim could not be ignored. She wanted Milton so she could have him stuffed and sit him at the dining room table, in full view of her neighbors as they passed by her picture window. By appearing to break bread with her nattily-dressed, if somewhat incommunicative companion, Mia hoped to derive a certain cachet from the fact that she now had a man in her house and was no longer dining alone. It was her hope that the sight of her masculine dinner companion would earn for her that extra measure of respect that might prompt her neighbours, with their frenetic Chihuahuas and Shih Tzus, to pass by her begonias and to cease using her lawn as the communal pissoir and plop place of choice. With a man in the house, she reasoned, one acquired a certain protective accoutrement of mystery and power.

Mia didn't really mind if Milton were a bit stiff and unresponsive as long as he looked reasonably life-like and fashionable from a distance. She did feel that stuffing him properly would be the biggest challenge. But, as she had had a class in taxidermy at School Night, where she successfully stuffed three skunks and an owl, she felt that she could cope nicely. After all, Milton was not that much different from a coyote or a skunk. He was merely somewhat bigger. And she also had a lifetime of stuffing Thanksgiving turkeys behind her.

However, as the crap-shoot progressed, minor sniping

Any Old Fart In A Storm

became a problem. Gerda began to quarrel with Trixie who only wanted Milton for a one-night stand - her ex-husband's wedding - and felt that, as undecomposed men were in short supply, no one should be afforded the luxury of Milton's companionship for more than an evening or two. In her view, Milton should be passed around like a Mongolian hot-pot and should be the property of all. No one person should be permitted to hog.

Jill was so desperate that she told Mia it was unfair and unreasonable of her to demand a full man when it was so obvious that she could clearly make do with a part. After all, Jill reasoned, Milton would only be seen at the table from the waist up. She considered this to be a flagrant and blatant waste of half a man. However, since the crap-shooting committee was unable to agree on a plan for utilizing the bottom of the body, it was decided that it would be impractical to sever Milton at the waist, and negotiations bogged down temporarily while someone went out for cokes.

Then, someone suggested that Mia was being stubborn and unreasonable as, it was pointed out, she could achieve her goal of heightened self-esteem more efficiently by placing the bottom half of Milton on a ladder in front of the window, thereby accomplishing her desired effect of impressing her neighbors with a masculine presence and, at the same time, freeing the top half of Milton for front-line duty elsewhere.

Trixie then argued that she could utilize the top half by sitting it in the limo and taking it to the wedding, but she would then have to explain why her date could not get out of the car. Thus, the feelings of the group, passionately presented to Gerda by the crap-shooting committee, were delineated and clarified and a conclusion reached: no one woman should be narcissistic enough to demand or expect the unrestricted right to hog a whole man.

Elizabeth Howkins

But Gerda countered that she held seniority by reason of age and degree of desperation and that she was entitled to a whole man. Her appeal was impassioned, buffered by examples of precedent both literary and legal that no princess in any fairy tale had ever gone to a ball with half a prince and that cutting up corpses was punishable by jail. Why, she demanded passionately, should she accept half a man anyway; after all, when she ordered a turkey, the butcher did not deliver a legless fowl. One expects a Christmas turkey to have all his salient parts and a Cornish hen to have two legs, so, it is not unreasonable, she argued, to expect a man to have a bottom and a top. Mia, drawing on her twenty years as a member of the bar, was then quick to point out the weaknesses in this analogy.

"Whenever you order a turkey or a chicken," she interjected smugly, "you never get the head."

"Look," said Trixie, "let's work this out. Men aren't exactly a dime a dozen. We can't turn on each other like a pack of starving wolverines. We are ladies, after all. Several of us have doctorates. Maybe Mia could get by with the bottom and I could manage with the top. Maybe, to prove that I am reasonable and willing to compromise, I could even get by with one arm provided it was night time and my escort didn't leave the car. After all, the wedding guests will only be viewing us from one side. I can wrap Milton's arm around my shoulder and, with my body strategically placed, I might even be able to conceal the absence of his head. Can anybody use the other arm?"

"Maybe Mia could get by with just one arm too by sitting on a couch in front of the picture window, so the neighbors can see an obviously masculine arm strung about her shoulders like a shawl," Gerda said, with a pretense at being helpful.

"You forgot one small problem," Jill said timidly.

Any Old Fart In A Storm

"What's that?" Trixie snorted.

"He won't have any head, only an arm, won't it look funny?"

"She won't need a head if she sits to the side of the couch," Trixie countered, never at a loss for ideas. "It will be assumed that his head is behind the wall. We all have to be flexible and bend a little."

"I've had it!" Mia shouted. "Flexibility has its limits. If you take away any more parts, I'll be left with an ear and a nose!"

At this point, Mabel, who had been unable to tag any viable parts, became desperate and offered to take Milton from the knees down. Trixie impulsively offered to settle for a foot. Just as the argument began to heat up, the doors of the I.C.U. opened behind them. Mia grabbed Nurse Mallet by the arm.

"Is it over yet?" she said.

"Oh no, dear, the most extraordinary thing has happened," Nurse Mallet said, waving a paper in front of Mia's face.

"What's that?"

"It's his breakfast order, dear, he filled it all out himself."

She began to read "...blueberry pancakes, no butter, sausage and bacon, two bagels, six eggs, over easy, three bowls of oatmeal..."

"Stop!" Mia screamed. "He's brain-dead. He can't order breakfast!"

"Sorry, dear, the machine malfunctioned. We made a little error. The deal is off. He isn't brain-dead at all. He was only drowsing. We'll be taking him off life support in a few days and he should be out of here in about a week just as good as new. I'm going out for a ciggie."

Nurse Mallet moved off down the hall. Not a word was spoken. Not a glance was exchanged. But somehow, through some finely-tuned extra-sensory camaraderie, they all knew at once exactly what had to be done. Gerda, their acknowledged leader, by reason of seniority of age and abrasiveness of tone, separated herself from the group and passed through the doors of the I.C.U. She presented herself as Milton's sister, come all the way from Pago Pago to buck him up with a chat. She slipped quietly into the cubicle and, in a supreme exercise of situation ethics, she calmly pulled the plug.

"*De minimus non curat lex* - the law does not concern itself with trifles," she muttered as she exited skilfully amid the clanging bells and buzzers, barely brushing the crash-cart with her designer jeans.

To Gilbert And George Or Who Needs Enemies?

Clive Murphy

1. *From an actress*

3 August

Tits, dogshit and more dogshit. There's Nice for you in a nutshell, darlings. Oh, and *winos* - lots and lots of them, pissed as farts, reading Simenon under the lauriers-roses (pink elephants?). Are you still on the wagon?

A bientôt,
Lallah

2. *From a failed writer, HIV positive, brave*

Thursday, August 5th

Dear G & G,

Writing this on, well not actually *on,* the Port Jetty. Gay Switchboard said I could come here and come here I have - three times in the last two hours. Who says Englishmen can't have multiple orgasms?

Sea defences - huge slabs of rock, cement etc. - have been chucked here higgledy-piggledy as if by Messrs Cyclopes on an off day. First you think you're alone. Then you become aware of nuderies and ruderies in every nook and cranny. A camp trio is cavorting under my very *nose*. One arrived all piratical with, believe me, a parrot on her shoulder. Another sported ribboned culottes and clutched a chihuahua. The third, in a sailor suit and a cloud of scent, was dragged into sight by two huskies - I'm sure she got the idea from Vogue.

My feet are *killing* me. Penetrated by the spines of sea urchins when I crawled down to bathe. *"Il faut plonger!"* screamed the trio, waving well manicured hands like windscreen-wipers. *"Vâches!"* I screamed back. "I *can't* dive! Why didn't you tell me sooner, you two-faced mother-fucking daughters of Gomorrah?" Much pouting of lips and heaving of shoulders. The parrot squawked and I distinctly saw the chihuahua wince.

That pink and white striped blazer I bought at Austin Reed's summer sale was a *succès fou* last night at Le Rusca where Jacques, the oh so dishy proprietor, dimmed up (is that the opposite of dimmed?) the lights to admire me. He's put N.Y. posters, mostly men in undies, on the walls and, in one corner, the statue of an uncircumcised peasant boy playing a flute.

Tonight it's wank-wank-suck-suck over the car park in the Boulevard Saint Jaures. Tomorrow the Cap de Nice by day and, by night, Le Blue Boy Disco. Isn't Gay Switchboard just a *mine* of information?

Forgive all this silliness. Be thankful you have one another and aren't Jewish.

Love
Ben

P.S. According to my phrase book, *'Je suis ici pour les affaires'* means 'I am here on business'.

PP.S. Has my absence from London left a gaping hole?

To Gilbert And George Or Who Needs Enemies?

3. *From a social worker*

Nice
12 August 1993

Dear Gilbert and George,

I am writing to you in layperson's terms about a matter which concerns me as a professional carer and as a human being. The letter is unofficial i.e. off the record.

Hilary Johnson has brought it to my notice that you employed her as a model during July. To be photographed so often and to be paid, however little, for her pains, has boosted her morale no end. In fact, she has begun to think of herself as quite a star. I shall not inform her Social Security Office of this transaction or they might query her allowance.

You do realise, don't you, that Hilary is not a boy? I only mention it because my No. 1 has advised me that your work so far has never depicted the female sex. I am pleased if you have consciously decided to break new ground. Women get a raw enough deal as it is without famous artists such as yourselves deciding to ignore them. Only the self-confidence the likes of you can instil in this future citizen will bring her round to a less rebellious attitude.

Needless to say, there is still much room for improvement. Strangers who don't realise, as we do, what a sweet girl she really is can react against her without mercy. Do you know Nice well? I imagine you do, given your work is represented here in a major museum. The other night I took her for a *boisson* to Le Pub Opéra at the corner of the rue St. François-de-Paule and the rue de la Terrasse and, whether because of her tattoos or her nodding to a rhythm on her Walkman, we were refused service. I doubt if that would happen in England. Still, it may have taught her a useful lesson. In her present

Clive Murphy

emotional state, though, it may equally have reinforced her bitterness because she has now started crunching her Coca Cola cans before she's even drained them of their contents. This is a sign I recognise of old and all I can do is spoil her a little, indulge her physical appetites e.g. her fondness for Chicken McNuggets and Chicken Cheeseburgers at McDonald's, for parachute lifts, water-skiing and wind-surfing in the bay. The parachute lifts are a real favourite. Imagine a motorboat dashing here and there dragging our Hilary aloft across the blue! At 200 francs a turn, three to four times a day, I'm glad it's not me that's paying. But I do think that the Social Services in offering these holidays to deprived youngsters are on the right track. Till we came to Nice I'd no idea Hilary was such a tomboy.

Please don't give up on this girl in the coming months. I mean, should you decide not yet to find a place for her in your pictures, might she help you to prepare and assemble your materials in the studio? Apart from your reputed generosity to AIDS victims, I know so little about you. Hilary is hale and hearty and in her adolescent prime. She trusts you and I'm sure you won't let her down. I have asked her to spend some of her pocket money on sending you a card.

> Yours respectfully,
> Pattie Purefoy
> Welfare Officer

4. *From a juvenile delinquent*

miss the Boys in prick lane spose patties OK in small dosus wish tho shed foRget heR sopeBox she pReechus even when shes plasteRd she nids a paRm tRee up heR Fanny
> see yeR
> Hil XOXO

To Gilbert And George Or Who Needs Enemies?

5. *From a fellow artist*

> Hôtel Massenet,
> Nice
> 18th August

Chers maîtres,

I note that your photo-piece 'Flower Worship' at the Musée d'Art Moderne is dated 1982. *Plus ça change.* What are your future plans? No more postcard collages, I hope. I always find them too close to my own territory for comfort. For my next 'Beachcomber' exhibition I've chosen the twelve or so *plages publiques* below the Promenade des Anglais. This evening the Plage du Centenaire yielded a baby's bottle, a doll's arm, a piece of elastoplast, a plastic cup, a French letter (unused, *arome vanille*), a Galeries Lafayette carrier-bag, a shoe, a pair of briefs and a copy of Nice-Matin whose front page advertises an appearance of Charles Aznavour (thought he was dead) in Golfe-Juan. Stick them on a beach mat, and Bob's your uncle: more 'conventional detritus transformed into ironic cultural statement' and another twelve thousand quid in the kitty. Not quite so pricey as your good selves, but then I don't work such long hours, do I? And I don't employ models or studio and secretarial assistants.

Does it ever occur to you that we're overpaid? Not a stone's throw from where I'm dining - the Mississippi - sorry, does the name distract you? - there are portrait artists, African drummers, fire-eaters, puppeteers and clowns working the shit out of themselves for a handful of francs. In the Marché aux Fleurs I've observed a first rate water-colourist who's lucky if he gets four hundred francs for a little masterpiece ... Have I made my point? I shall shortly be driving to Cannes to pit some of my ill-gotten gains against the croupiers of Jimmy Z's.

Have I doubly made my point?

Given your own all too sound financial position, I cannot understand why you refused to join me here if only for a couple of days. Don't you ever give your earning power a rest? Do you dress in those prissy, buttoned-up suits because you're inwardly busy playing bank tellers counting your estimated and actual earnings?

Frankly, I'm finding our friendship rather one-sided. You won't gamble. You won't read or go to exhibitions* for fear of being influenced. Perhaps you won't even take a short holiday with me away from that gloomy, shuttered house of yours because, you are afraid that, if you stopped to think, you might die of shame. Or are you afraid that the purity of the Riviera light might expose you for what you are, careerists seeking maximum publicity, male Madonnas in sheep's clothing? I can't, for much longer, endure your joylessness, your lack of warmth. I wonder if your wide-eyed good manners are no more than the snobby detachment of two insufferable prigs pretending to be naive when they're merely naff.

Yours, you'll decide, in envy and self-loathing,
Rupert

*You attend your own, of course. You'll be dropping by at Peking or Shanghai when your 'work' goes on show there next month, won't you? Why, by the way, should I have to learn about all this from my dealer? Why are you so fucking cautious with *me* ? Very Chinese of you. I've no doubt whatever that in China you'll go down a bomb - personally at least.

To Gilbert And George Or Who Needs Enemies?

6. *From a lounge lizard*

> Hôtel de la Gloire,
> Place Masséna,
> 06000 - Nice
> Saturday

How wise of you to remain aestivating in Spitalfields. Awoke, Morning One, to find myself twice bitten - great purple blotches on neck and shoulder. *"Les méduses!"* cried the femme de chambre. "Since when have jellyfish been a hazard of your hotel?" I protested. Whereupon she became coquettish, then jokey: "Lovebites? ... Vampires?"

> Be good,
> Fergus

Tell Clyde and Phyllis that *filet de St. Pierre rôti et sa fondue de tomates au basilic* are as nothing compared with their Market Caff's good old r.b. and Yorkshire pud.

I'm in the devil of a fix as usual. Please, please, please send me the sterling equivalent of FF.8,000 as soon as ever poss. I'll try to repay you mid-September. Take this as an IOU.

7. *From an educator*

> Nice
> 27.8.93

Hi Gilbert! Hi George!

Gwen joins me in thanking you for allowing us to share your superb collection of ornaments and icons and for wining and

Clive Murphy

dining us so royally afterwards at your local Music Hall. How fortunate you are to have this wonderful reminder of pre-war England in a predominantly Moslem district. What do your Bengali neighbours make of 'Down at the Old Bull and Bush' and 'Knock 'em in the Old Kent Road'? And why don't we see more Bengalis in your work? Forgive the latter question. Perhaps they've refused you or else you've a *coup de peinture* in store for us. Not that 'peinture' is quite the right word, is it? You don't paint in any accepted sense, just as it's no secret that you can't draw.

You mentioned that several of your acquaintances would be in Nice at the same time as ourselves. We have not, to our knowledge, met any of them. What a pity you didn't provide us with letters of introduction. You also mentioned that your 'Flower Worship' is on display at the Gallery of Modern and Contemporary Art. My wife enjoyed it more than I. I do not respond to your choice of color. As a matter of fact I'd have expected, rather, to find an example of your *oeuvre* at the Naive Art Gallery. I consider your outlook and execution essentially simplistic.

You told us how your relations with the established church have been tarnished by the opinions of a former rector of your parish who thinks of you both, despite or because of your Christian references, as pornographers and blasphemers. I reject this crude assessment. I regard you as deeply religious. Indeed I feel it my duty, in view of your great wealth, to point out that, here in Nice on the hill of Cimiez, a Biblical Message Center has been built to house the seventeen Chagall paintings inspired by the books of Genesis and Exodus and by the Song of Songs, which the artist and his wife donated to the French Nation in 1966. I can vouch that it is a place of tranquility and that its atmosphere engenders peace and spiritual calm in the hearts of visitors with many of whom Gwen and I communed.

To Gilbert And George Or Who Needs Enemies?

Surely it is not beyond the bounds of practicality that you persuade some future rector to let you do the same for Christchurch, Spitalfields? This might help to mitigate the effects of the predicted race wars in the area and to lay the evil shade of Jack the Ripper. You must also design some stained-glass windows. I know that Hawksmoor 'were he living at this hour' would not disapprove. Chagall expressly designed stained-glass windows for the concert hall of his Center, and I gather Christchurch is already used for Musical Festivals as well as for Evangelical Christian Worship. I should mention that the Center is at present holding an exhibition of 12th to 19th Century Byzantine and Post-Byzantine Icons. Given you are iconologists, whether as investors or lovers of a genre or both, I suggest you read *L'Icône* by Michel Quenot. It is not unusual, I hear, for exhibitions with a religious theme to run in tandem with the permanent Chagall collection. I can see no reason why your own lovely home in Fournier Street might not become a public shrine in tandem with your church.

But I speak of years and years ahead. In terms of your true potential you are still crawling in the nursery: before handing in your dinner pail you must develop and mature.

Meanwhile, Gwen and I bless your endeavours, present and future. This letter is our last while vacationing in Europe. Tomorrow we fly back to Wichita where my students await me. Please remember these 'two old fogeys' in your prayers as we shall remember you. Always follow the paths of goodness rather than self-righteousness. Always use your talent to assuage the suffering of humanity at large.

Yours in Christian love,
Arthur and Gwen

You have our home address. Don't wait till Christmas to reply. Write to us in detail in the Fall.

CONTRIBUTORS

IVY BANNISTER was born in New York but has been living in Dublin since 1970. She won the Mobil Ireland Playwrighting Award in 1993 and the Hennessy Award for short fiction, and has a collection *Magician* ready for publication. Her story first appeared in Panurge 21(*Debatable Lands*) 1994.

JONATHAN CHAMBERLAIN is a London writer aged 37. He has had three stories in *London Magazine* and three in *Panurge*. *Harold* first appeared in Panurge 6, 1987.

WILLIAM CHARLTON is Head of Philosophy at Edinburgh University. Born in 1935 he has been in various Fontana anthologies, co-written a biography of Arthur Machen and published a book on aesthetics. His story first appeared in Panurge 6.

KEN CLAY is 56 and lives in Warrington. A former reviewer for the *Morning Star,* he has published fiction in David Craig's *Fireweed*. He has also worked for thirty years as a chemical engineer. *Decline And Fall* first saw light in Panurge 4, 1986.

NORMAN HARVEY is an ex-civil servant living in Wiltshire. He has won the Dimbleby Prize and the Gooding Award for short stories. His story also appeared in Panurge 4.

ELIZABETH HOWKINS lives in Bryn Mawr, USA and is married to a psychiatrist. She was a prizewinner in the Stand Short Story Competition 1993 (judges Susan Hill and John Murray). Her story will appear in Panurge 23, 1995.

PHILIP SIDNEY JENNINGS was born in Weymouth and has spent time in Jamaica and the USA. He did an MA in Creative Writing in New York and has had stories in *Sunk Island Review, Penthouse, Encounter, Punch* and the *Evening Standard*. In 1992 his teenage novel *Dome* appeared. He teaches writing in the City Literary Institute and is doing research in Creative Writing at Lancaster. He was born in 1946. His story first came out in Panurge 21,1994.

CLIVE MURPHY has published seven recorded autobiographies by various people living in the East End, two with Secker and five with Dobson. He also published three novels with Dobson in the Seventies: *Summer Overtures, Freedom For Mr Mildew* and *Nigel Someone*. His story will appear in Panurge 23.

JOHN MURRAY founded Panurge magazine in 1984 and edited it until 1987. He then resumed editorship (from David Almond) at the start of 1993. His stories have been in the *London Review of Books, London Magazine, Literary Review, Irish Press, Fiction Magazine, Stand Magazine, Sunk Island Review* and *Panurge* . His collection *Pleasure* appeared with Aidan Ellis in 1987 and won the Dylan Thomas Award in 1988. His story here appeared in Panurge 18, 1993.

ÉILÍS NÍ DHUIBHNE was born in 1954 and lives near Dublin. Her collections *Blood And Water* (1988) and *Eating Women Is Not Recommended* (1991) both came out with Attic Press. Her novel *The Bray House* appeared with Attic in 1990. She also writes books for children which have been shortlisted for various awards. She is a scholar of Old Irish, and is married to a Professor of Irish. Her story first appeared in Panurge 2, 1985 and was anthologised in *Best Short Stories 1986*.

JAMES WADDINGTON was born in 1942, has worked in Zambia and West Cumbria and now lives just outside Huddersfield. He has been in *Best Short Stories 1991*, *The Minerva Book Of Stories*, *Sunk Island Review* and *Panurge* three times. This story first appeared in Panurge 20.

STEPHEN WADE teaches Literature and Media at North Lindsey College, Scunthorpe. He has written on Heaney and Isherwood and his fiction has been on Radio 3 and elsewhere. *Churwell Poems* came out with Littlewood in 1987. He is currently working on a study of Philip Roth. *Abe Poge* first appeared in Panurge 2.